HER IMPOSSIBLE
BABY BOMBSHELL

HER IMPOSSIBLE
BABY BOMBSHELL

DANI COLLINS

MILLS & BOON

First published in Great Britain 2021
by Mills & Boon, an imprint of HarperCollins*Publishers* Ltd,
1 London Bridge Street, London, SE1 9GF

www.harpercollins.co.uk

HarperCollins*Publishers*
1st Floor, Watermarque Building,
Ringsend Road, Dublin 4, Ireland

Large Print edition 2021

Her Impossible Baby Bombshell © 2021 Dani Collins

ISBN: 978-0-263-28891-9

09/21

MIX
Paper from
responsible sources
FSC® C007454

This book is produced from independently certified
FSC™ paper to ensure responsible forest management.
For more information visit www.harpercollins.co.uk/green.

Printed and bound in Great Britain
by CPI Group (UK) Ltd, Croydon, CR0 4YY

For my son, Sam,
who takes it in stride when his mother
texts him out of the blue asking,
"Why would a young man your age
get a vasectomy?" and later brainstorms
some scenes with me when I'm stuck.
Thanks, dude. You're the best.

PROLOGUE

LOVE. *YUCK.* IVY LAM was over it.

She wasn't cynical by nature, but she'd only come to this engagement party to be polite. A DM to an old work colleague asking if she could buy him coffee to discuss a career shift had resulted in the invitation from Kevin.

If you're in town, come to our party. Lots of leads will be there.

So she'd picked up a bottle of wine and spent way too much money on a dress. It was a "casual" afternoon barbecue in one of Vancouver's most upscale neighborhoods, celebrating a society engagement, but she needed to make a good first impression on potential employers. Easy-peasy.

She had settled on a dusty pink knee-length floral dress that had a 1950s Sunday school vibe to it, but the darts and pleats gave it a tailored look and the scooped neckline made the most of her modest bosom.

For all the good the effort had done her. Most of the women were in daring halter tops with bohemian skirts and eyelet sundresses that hugged their curves. Ivy was both a sore thumb that stuck out and a wallflower to be overlooked.

It was the story of her life. Ivy was neither an introvert nor an extrovert. She was middle-of-the-road, which made her too boring to be the center of attention but perfect for filling out background laughter.

Kevin had been right about the guest list, though. It was brimming with Vancouver's top commercial real estate developers, stock traders and financial investors. Even a real, live billionaire—if the hushed remark she'd overheard was to be believed.

Tsai Jun Li was—well, it didn't matter that he'd made her blood heat when Kevin had seemed to make a point of introducing them. Ivy wasn't here to find a man.

Therefore, it hadn't bothered her a bit that Jun Li had been drawn away seconds later by a stacked blonde. Blondie was welcome to him. Ivy refused to get hung up on a man who didn't want her. Not again.

Even if he might be, without exaggeration, the most beautiful man she'd ever seen.

No. Either way she sliced it, there was nothing here for her. Trying to network at such a celebratory event would be tasteless and Kevin's effusive love for Carla only reminded Ivy of how spectacularly she had failed when it came to happily-ever-after.

Thirty minutes after she arrived, she quietly exited the Point Grey mansion without saying goodbye. As she emerged onto the stoop, the April sunshine made her sneeze.

Allergic to love, she almost said to the valet who blessed her.

"I'm ordering a ride share," she said in answer to his offer to fetch her car.

She didn't hurry to bring up the app, though. She wasn't anxious to go back to her father's. His new relationship was also loving and sincere and hard to be around. Ivy was happy for him, but she felt like a dupe for believing she had had anything like it.

What a waste! But no more kidding herself. She was moving on. That's what this trip was about.

She went down the steps to stand in the shade of an ornamental plum tree, trying to read her email. She was hoping for an impromptu request for an interview, but there was nothing because it was Saturday afternoon and the sun was shining. The entire city was outside enjoying a startlingly beautiful and unseasonably warm spring day.

Ivy stepped into the sun and turned her face up, letting the warmth and brightness shine down on her with all its might. She was coming home. It wasn't so much a do-over as the launch of a new and improved Ivy. One who wasn't so gullible. One who made her own decisions. Bold, self-serving ones.

"It's false advertising," a male voice said.

The valet made an "eep" noise and said,

"The Pagani?" He snatched up a key from his board and hurried away.

Ivy looked up the steps, and there *he* stood, surveying her the way an emperor assessed his domain.

According to Kevin, the thirtyish Chinese billionaire had been his "roommate from our time at UBC." That made Jun Li sound very tame when he actually moved like a predator, gliding down the stairs in a panther-like lope.

Ivy didn't mean to stare, but seriously, she forgot to breathe, he was so good-looking.

He had short black hair with just enough length on top to be rakish. His brows were stern, his beard trimmed to a thin line that framed his square jaw and somber mouth. His cheekbones were so high and sharp, they should have shattered the screen on her phone. His skin held a warm golden hue set off by the lime-green color of his pullover.

How was that loosely knit but closely worn sweater not wearing him?

Ivy only noticed his clothes because they so elegantly hugged his muscled shoulders and accentuated his athletic build. He'd skimmed up his sleeves to reveal his forearms, adding to his air of being utterly unaware of how stunning he was. He was like a snapshot out of a men's magazine. He only needed to tuck a hand into his bone-colored chinos and point at something off camera.

What would he look like in his underwear, she wondered sinfully.

He kept coming toward her, and her admiration sharpened to something more visceral. A tightness of danger with a thrill of excitement.

Lust.

It was a testament to how anemic her last relationship had been that she had never experienced anything like this surge of anticipation for the man she had wanted to marry, but heat built in her throat as Jun Li closed in on her.

Just as she wondered if he would overwhelm her completely, he stopped in the shade of the tree.

"The weather," he clarified. His mouth might

have twitched as though he was laughing at how mesmerized she was. "An arctic outflow will come through tomorrow and kill all these flowers." He nodded at the planter pots filled with cheerful pansies. "Or a pineapple express from Hawaii will dump a metric ton of rain and drown them. Everyone who visits thinks this is what it's like to live here. It's not."

He was making her feel exactly how she didn't want to feel—like a tongue-tied adolescent with her first crush. Like a woman who allowed men to tell her things she already knew. She wanted to be one of those sophisticates like that blonde who hadn't been afraid to make a play for a man who was clearly out of her league.

"I know" was all she managed to say. "I grew up here."

His brows went up slightly. "I misunderstood. I thought Kevin said he knew you from his time in Hong Kong."

"We worked together there, yes."

Kevin had a very similar background to Ivy's middle-class, second-generation immigrant upbringing. As a fellow Chinese Canadian boosting a banking career with a stint in Hong Kong, he'd taken her under his wing for the year she'd worked in his department, offering her a sibling-like bond of outward teasing and underlying support.

"I took his job when he left." That felt very braggy, but she was trying to overcome years of allowing herself to be reduced. "Six months ago, I took a transfer to Toronto." Huge mistake careerwise, but at least it had forced her to confront how poorly she was allowing herself to be treated and put a stop to it once and for all. "My father still lives here, so I'm moving back to enjoy the smooth traffic and affordable cost of living. Fabulous weather is not this city's only selling feature," she punctuated with a facetious smile.

"I would have sworn it had none, but I stand corrected." His mouth curled with equal irony. The flick of his gaze to her shoes and back suggested male notice. The crinkles beside his eyes suggested he appreciated what he saw. "Do you need a lift?" he asked as a growling engine approached.

Her heart skipped, and she thought, *This is it. This is what it's like to be single.*

The tendrils of attraction within her were sliding and coiling with possibility. A flattered blush warmed her cheeks, and she felt the rush of preparing to take a big leap.

At the last second, old habits had her stupid mouth stammering, "I'm in Richmond. It's too far out of your way." Because he couldn't possibly want to spend a second longer with her than he had to. This was exactly how she'd wound up in a dead-end long-distance relationship for *eight years.*

"I'm looking for an excuse to drive," he said as a cobalt-blue convertible roadster stopped before him. It was a two-seater with fins and muscles and spoked hubcaps. There was a hawklike beak down the hood. The windshield was slanted to an acute, aerodynamic angle, and the mirrors swept out like antennae.

Ivy couldn't help biting her lip in temptation. "It looks like something a crime-fighting duo would use to chase supervillains."

"Blame me for the crime rate, then. I forgot I owned it. I had to have it tuned up before I could drive it, but now that I have, I've decided to ship it home. I'm hardly ever here." He opened the passenger door. "Are you really going to make me save the city all by myself?"

Ivy stifled a snort at anyone owning a car like this—likely worth seven figures—and not only forgetting about it, but having it sent around the world like an overnight package.

This man was not only out of her league, he was from a different planet. But when would she get a chance like this again?

"If the city *needs* us…" She dropped into the low-slung seat, feeling like a racecar driver must. She dug in her bag for her sunglasses, a cheap pair of cat-eyes that she'd grabbed while picking out this dress.

He put on a pair of designer wraparounds that made him look even more sexy and inscrutable. As he pulled away, she felt like one of those daring women who got on the back of the bad boy's motorcycle. She felt sexy and self-possessed just by being next to him in this wicked car on this glorious day.

They wound down the hill through tree-lined streets, but when he reached the main road that would have taken them south, there was a detour arrow.

"This looks like a sign," he said.

"Are you being literal? Or do you mean it's a warning that I shouldn't move back here because this is what I'll be up against?"

"I'm saying we're being offered a chance to seize this rare, fine day. How do you feel about taking the long way home?"

She waved her hand, silently deferring to him, bemused that she was here at all.

He proved his familiarity with the side streets, and they were soon across the bridge and skirting English Bay, heading into Stanley Park. From there, he took the Lion's Gate bridge and ran through the gears up the Sea to Sky highway.

Her skirt fluttered as he picked up speed.

Her heart pressed back into her spine and her hair snapped her cheeks. She grinned with delight as the music blared and he smoothly whistled past sedans and minivans. It was a sensation of absolute freedom and she should have let them both enjoy it, but she wound up ruining it.

"You know they'll impound this car if you go too far over the speed limit?"

"They'll have to catch me first," he said cockily, but he eased off a little, glancing at his speed and the sign they passed.

"I've been working in compliance," she said by way of apology. "Job hazard."

"You're still in banking?"

"Yes." She understood he was asking because Kevin had left the bank in Hong Kong to take a private-sector position in asset management here in Vancouver. "What do you do?" She had an idea but wondered how a man like him answered such a question.

"The bulk of my work involves international infrastructure projects. We have a lot of contracts around the Belt Road Initiative.

I'm president of a conglomerate with a diverse portfolio, though. My father started it with medical devices, and we're still a global manufacturer for those. My aunt has a handbag supply chain that does ridiculously well."

"Why is it ridiculous? Every woman needs something trendy in which to carry her husband's wallet."

It was a silly joke, a dig toward all the men who complained about holding purses in shopping malls but didn't want to carry their own wallet.

Jun Li's expression grew more alert. "I assumed you were single because you were at the party alone."

Whose wallet do you carry? he seemed to be asking.

A man who led me on for years and never really wanted me. That wallet has been sent to the secondhand store.

A worldly woman with confidence in her own worth didn't blurt out a sob story about being taken for granted and rejected, though.

"I'm consciously uncoupled as of last

Christmas," she said in the most laissez-faire tone she could manage. "You?"

"Consciously uncoupled as a lifestyle choice."

"Ah. Noted," she said dryly, hearing the underlying warning. It stung more than it should, but she was still raw from her breakup. She didn't need another man telling her she wasn't good enough for forever. Kudos to Jun Li for being up front about it, at least.

She made herself enjoy the moment and they were halfway to Whistler before she realized it.

"How far are we going?" he asked and her heart lurched as the words 'all the way' sprang into her mind.

She didn't have the nerve to say it and he wound up taking the next exit off the highway. It led to a tourist attraction with a gondola to summit and a dining lodge.

"I've never gone up there. Have you?"

"No."

"Is today the day?"

"When will we have another?"

Minutes later, they were ambling along an

interpretive path enjoying spectacular views of the mountains and the sound below.

"I don't care if it is false advertising," Ivy said as she stood at the rail of a platform that jutted out into thin air. "When it's beautiful, it's really beautiful. To me, that's worth suffering the bad days."

"I'd rather avoid the bad days and accept the good ones as the gift they are." He turned to her.

He wanted to kiss her. She knew it and she wanted that, too. She turned and lifted her gaze to meet his. They were both smiling.

She didn't let herself wonder what any of it meant. This day was a gift for both of them.

When his mouth settled on hers, lips firm and smooth and hot, her whole body grew charged with electricity.

This was her chance to take another step toward moving on, she realized with a flash of possibility. Indulging herself with Jun Li was liable to wipe her memory clean all the way back to her first kiss in grade school, but that was exactly what she needed.

The conscientious woman inside her, the one still longing for love, marriage and a baby carriage, warned that a man like him could set a bar that no other man could reach. He could destroy her without even meaning to.

She told that fearmongering voice to pipe down and kissed him back.

They kissed until they were both breathless. When he lifted his head, she discovered they were pressed together, arms wrapped tight around each other.

He licked his lips.

"How do you feel about being used in a rebound situation?" she asked before she could think twice.

"I feel great about it." His expression relaxed into one of sensual anticipation. "I leave tomorrow morning." His eyes narrowed as he gauged her reaction to that.

"So do I."

"Let's enjoy this day, then."

CHAPTER ONE

Four months later, Singapore

EXACTLY AS SHE had back in April, Ivy accepted a flute of champagne with no intention of drinking it, even though her mouth was a desert. She held the glass to blend in while she got her bearings at a party where she only knew one person.

Actually, zero. Her quarry wasn't here yet. She gave the dimly lit piano bar another nervous skim of her gaze—as if Jun Li was a man anyone could miss.

She belonged even less at this five-star Singapore hotel than she had at Kevin's party. Jun Li's guests were VPs and CEOs whose net incomes made Kevin's circle look like burger flippers at a fast food joint.

Instead of her prim pink dress, she wore a

cheongsam-inspired sheath with cap sleeves, its red shoulders fading to indigo at the knee-length hem. Was it noticeably tight around her middle? Yes, but it had always served her well at the banking functions she was forced to attend, so she'd worn it as a security blanket.

She had hoped it would work for what was essentially a corporate event, but it was too demure for a trophy wife and not chic enough for a female executive with stock options. Any minute she expected a caterer to hand her a tray of canapés and ask her to serve them to table five.

Everything about this was *awful*. She was bordering on stalking, coming all this way to ambush a man in front of his employees, but in the three weeks since she'd discovered her pregnancy, she'd had little luck reaching out through normal channels. Jun Li hadn't given her his number, and his privacy settings on social media were locked down tight. A gauntlet of personal assistants and low-level managers had fobbed her off and shut her down, clearly judging her a schemer of some kind. She'd even asked a headhunter to nose around for jobs that might grant her an interview with him, but that process took forever, and this felt urgent. For both of them.

Truth was, she was still in shock and denial, somehow convinced it wouldn't be real until she told Jun Li. She had to tell him before she revealed it to anyone else, but getting to him was nearly impossible.

She had resorted to calling Kevin. Aside from sending a wedding gift and regrets, she'd been avoiding him, not wanting to know whether Jun Li had told him they'd spent a night together. She wasn't ashamed of their brief affair, but it was private. She'd done it for herself and wanted it to be a special memory that was between the two of them. She wasn't up for any teasing over it. She wasn't running around bragging that she'd bagged a billionaire. She'd be devastated if Jun Li was boasting about conquering her.

With all other avenues exhausted, however, she had screwed up her courage and invited

Kevin for coffee, supposedly to discuss her career.

"You haven't found the right fit yet?" he asked with surprise.

"I've been offered a position, but I'd like your take. I don't know if it will be flexible enough in the long run." That was true enough. Her entire life was changing, and she needed a position that would adapt to the needs of a single mother.

They sat down a few days later and warmed up with small talk about his upcoming wedding. It provided the perfect opening to bring up her real reason for seeing him.

"Who's your best man? Jun Li?" She already knew he wasn't.

"My brother. Jun Li can't make it. Annual strategy meeting in Singapore." Kevin had set down his coffee to side-eye her. "Why? Were you hoping to see him again? Carla thinks you two hooked up because you both left our party early."

Ivy suffered an appalled moment of realizing she was being gossiped about, but it was obviously a joke. He didn't really believe they had connected.

"Oh yeah, right," Ivy scoffed after the longest, most agonizingly culpable silence. She hoped he read her nervous, blushing laughter as unrequited attraction, not guilt. "Every woman was throwing herself at him, but Tsai Jun Li, the Chinese *billionaire*, went home with *me*. Five minutes after we met." She added an eye roll to really sell how outrageous the suggestion was.

Whether Kevin believed her or not, she didn't know. She didn't have the nerve to look him in the eye after that.

She should have confessed all and admitted, *I really need help*, but it felt like a gross breach of ethics to air one man's private business to another.

After a moment, he had said, "You could do worse. You *have* done worse." His voice was a lot more compassionate than his words. He knew all about her woes with Bryant.

Kevin had segued into asking about the job

she'd been offered, and Ivy lost her chance to ask how Jun Li might react to her news.

She knew how he was going to react—with complete and utter disbelief. That's why this felt like such a personal, delicate matter that needed to be discussed in person. A text or voice mail wouldn't convince him and ran the risk of an assistant getting the news first.

If this wrap-up party had been more difficult to sleuth out, Ivy might have gone back to Kevin, but things had fallen into place very easily. The itinerary for the entire week had been on the corporate website, including the fact Jun Li was scheduled to present some awards tonight, recognizing the most innovative suggestions from the week's meetings.

Ivy had extended the start date for her new job in Vancouver, finished moving and used points to book a package, arriving in Singapore yesterday.

At least she was getting a final vacation before settling into single motherhood, she thought dourly as she glared into her flattening champagne. Because it was looking as though Jun Li wouldn't even show up—

A stir in the crowd brought her head up. She glimpsed him through the throng, and her heart stalled. Her knees went soft. She shifted so she had a better view of him, and her shoulders tensed so hard with nerves and jubilation, she could hardly breathe.

He seemed to stop time, pausing to survey the milling guests. He was still the most beautiful man Ivy had ever seen, and it was his superpower to seem completely unaware of his impact. In this faux candlelight, his complexion held a godlike bronze sheen. He wore a striped shirt, open at the collar, and a pair of tailored pants with a cuff, casually elegant and completely untouchable. Beyond her.

How had this pregnancy even happened? That's what she was thinking as her shoes from the outlet mall pinched her feet and a woman approached him, curvaceous and stunning in a peacock-blue cocktail dress and an abundance of jewelry that Ivy instinctively knew was real.

Ivy couldn't compete with that. Her gaze glued itself to him as she waited for him to notice her, half terrified, half thrilled to merely be in his orbit again while her heart tripped over itself with jealousy and loss. Her instinct was to crawl away. The last thing she wanted was a humiliating rejection in front of all these people.

If only she could take heart from the fact Jun Li's aloof expression didn't change as he spoke to that other woman, but she'd found him very hard to read when she'd spent an afternoon and evening with him. As it turned out, he'd been seducing her the whole time, so he might be doing the same to that woman right now for all she knew. Perhaps he already had.

A small choke of agony left her at the thought. She felt tangled in barbed wire as she stood there. She wanted to rush away and hide, but if he was romantically involved with anyone, he ought to know what *she* knew.

There would be no convenient time to approach him. No easy way to say what had to be said. She had come all this way, and it was time to wade in before he was completely surrounded or disappeared.

As she started forward, her situation hit her as very tawdry. Not the one-night stand part. She had agreed to that and, even though it had stung that he hadn't made any effort to reach out to her afterward, she accepted their time together as merely a fling.

No, the fact they'd been intimate but she was forced to go to these lengths so he could disbelieve and disregard her was eating her alive.

She was so focused on Jun Li, a touch on her arm made her jolt in surprise. A young man gave her a pained smile. "You're not on the list."

She could only stare blankly. He repeated it in Mandarin.

"You don't know who I am," she said, using her own flawless Mandarin.

"Exactly. I know every face except yours. Can you come with me, please?"

"No, I—" She glanced at Jun Li, digging in her heels. His attention was turned on that other woman, and he wasn't even looking this way.

"Please don't make a scene," the young man said. His hand on her arm firmed.

Ivy had the panicked feeling of someone being pulled beneath the surface of a lake, certain she was about to drown.

She yanked her arm free and hissed, "Go tell him Kevin Chow's friend Ivy needs five minutes."

Dropping Kevin's name gave the young man pause. After a wavering second, he said, "Wait by the elevator."

She did, begrudgingly, and watched as he went to Jun Li to speak in his ear.

Jun Li's head came up. His gaze seemed to hit her like a spear from across the room, deafening her to the din of conversation and the patter of piano keys. She couldn't read anything in his body language. Was he pleased? Appalled? She didn't know, but a hot sting of adrenaline shot to the ends of her fingers and toes, urging her to run while another part of her melted under his gaze.

She didn't understand why she reacted to him this way, and it was ten times stronger now they had shared a night of passion. *More.*

Her hand twitched, wanting to protectively cover her middle, but that would be far too telling when people were turning their heads, picking up on where his attention had gone.

Jun Li flicked his hand in an unspoken, *I'll handle it.* He left his group and wove unerringly toward her, expression inscrutable.

As he closed in, her lungs compressed and her insides began to tremble. His profound effect on her was not the thrill of catching a handsome, powerful man's attention. It was a painful sting of raw fear because she sensed his irritation at her turning up this way.

This was a far more daunting man than the one she'd met in Vancouver—which she hadn't realized was possible—but he still made her blood move like lava under her skin. Instead of basking in the glow of his attention, however, she felt spotted by an eagle. Picked apart. Naked.

It struck her that she'd gone to these ridiculous lengths so she could experience the soaring feeling of being in his presence again, but that had been a mistake. He was about to shoot her down, and the fall would be crippling.

"Ivy." There was no warmth in his voice. There was no hostility, either, which made it worse. He conveyed annoyance that she was bothering him at work, but otherwise he was indifferent to her being here.

She had the sudden, horrifying sense that he wouldn't have remembered her at all if she hadn't just given her name to his PA.

It was a plunge into reality from a fantasy she hadn't acknowledged. Deep down, she had imagined he might want to see her again. How incredibly foolish of her. He was supposed to have *cured* her of yearning for a man to bolster her sense of self-worth.

She cut off her anguished thoughts. The

backs of her eyes were hot, and her throat wanted to close, but she forced herself to adopt her boardroom demeanor, the one she used when she had to deliver bad news. She was the person on staff everyone loved to resent. She had learned to wear a dispassionate veil to protect herself.

"I'm sorry to bother you," she said in a level voice. "It was difficult to reach you without revealing why I need to speak with you. It's a personal matter."

His brows came together with genuine concern. "Kevin?"

"No."

Just as quickly, comprehension washed over his expression along with weary cynicism. "If I gave you a wrong impression when we—"

"You didn't." She'd done that to herself and would scream her mortification into a pillow later. "I only need five minutes, but I have information you should have. It's private," she added as his assistant hovered behind him.

Jun Li drew a skeptical breath, looking like he wanted to rebuff her, but his gaze flickered over her. She was watching him so closely, trying so hard to read him, she caught the flash of something—memory? Hunger?

Whatever it was disappeared so quickly, it left a void inside her the way a detonation left a scorched crater in the earth.

He withdrew a card from his pocket and loomed close to her.

She was so disconcerted, so buffeted by his dynamic energy, she took a step back, not realizing he was only touching the call button near her hip. She practically fell through the doors when they opened behind her.

He caught her arm to steady her. "I'll escort you down." He guided her into the empty elevator and shook his head when the young man would have joined them. "How did you get up here?" he asked her as the doors closed.

By riding the elevator until she was motion sick and slipping into the ladies' room ages before the greeters with their tablets and their gift bags had arrived. "Does it matter?"

"It's my hotel. I'd like to know how my security was bypassed, yes." He touched his card to the panel.

His hotel. Right. He wasn't just some guy she'd slept with. He was the head of a Chinese infrastructure conglomerate with projects and investments worldwide. He didn't have time for a lowly one-night stand to bend his ear. She ignored his question to blurt what she had come to say.

"Look, I know my coming here seems extreme, but—"

The floor didn't drop. It went up, causing her to stagger again.

"Are you all right?" He frowned, and his hand returned to her elbow.

"I thought you were taking me downstairs."

"I will. You said this was a private matter." The doors opened almost immediately. He escorted her across a small foyer into a two-story mansion of a penthouse.

It was the kind of over-the-top luxury she'd only seen in reality shows about the rich and famous. He walked her down a spiral staircase made of glass into a living area where the wall of windows looked onto the colorful lights of Singapore against the night sky.

She was completely taken aback by the astonishing view and understated opulence of white leather sofas arranged to enjoy a fireplace that peeked through to an elegant dining room. There were modern art sculptures and abstracts on the walls, an area rug that had to be silk and chandeliers that had to be crystal.

"Drink?" he invited.

"I can't, thank you." She cleared her throat and dug deep in search of the woman she'd pretended to be that day with him. Experienced. Detached. This was a compliance error, she reminded herself. That's all. "I'm not here to attempt an extension of our..." Relationship? "Association," she decided in a strained voice. "I only thought you should know that I'm pregnant."

Her heart pounded so hard, she thought the whole building must be pulsating with the sound. Her skin felt hot, but clammy with sweat.

His expression didn't change. "Congratulations?"

"It's yours."

His breath hissed out in a humorless snort while his shoulders slanted with fatalism. He gave a small shake of his head that asked *Why are you wasting my time?*

"Hear me out." She held up a hand, noticed it was trembling and tucked it under her elbow, folding her arms defensively. "I broke up with my boyfriend last Christmas. You're the only man I've been with since. Does this look like a full-term pregnancy to you?" She opened her arms to indicate the subtle curve in her middle.

It was nearing the end of July. She was seventeen weeks along, looking more like she'd been indulging at an all-inclusive buffet than pregnant.

"Whether you're pregnant or not I couldn't say…" His attention traversed all over her, like a paintbrush making several long, thorough strokes to leave a thick coat. When he dragged his gaze back to hers, his was sparking with heat that was smothered with cynicism. "You're not the first woman to make a claim like this, you know. They don't usually have the information I confided to *you*—"

"Don't," she warned, heart wrenched by the contempt she could hear in his tone. The one that censured her against being desperate and foolish. The one that said she had grossly overstepped by coming here.

She was used to powerful men dismissing her. The truth was often inconvenient, but this wasn't a gray area in a policy or regulation that she was suggesting he abide by. It was way more personal than that. And even though she'd known he would react this way, it hurt to be accused of dishonesty. She might tell white lies, but she was dead honest when it came to life, death and tax implications.

She swallowed and hugged herself again.

"I'm not here to ask for money or a ring. I'm telling you because it's information you deserve to have. I'm perfectly capable of raising this baby on my own and plan to."

"Great. Consider me informed. I'll escort you to your room."

It was a bluff. She could tell he was testing her resolve to see how she would react to such a callous dismissal.

She wanted to cry. Everything about this was going exactly as she had expected—except for the fact he had the power to cut her in half with a few dispassionate words. She wouldn't beg him to believe her, though.

"I'm not staying here." She spoke with as much poise as she could muster, biting back pointing out his hotel was way beyond her budget.

"I'll ask the doorman to cover your taxi fare, then." He waved at the stairs.

"That's not necessary," she murmured, hesitating.

She wanted to ask one more thing, but it was such a blood-chilling worry, she could barely give voice to it.

His brows went up with exaggerated patience. A muscle pulsed in his jaw, betraying he was finding this interaction disturbing. He was probably already thinking he ought to take a test to be sure and probably annoyed with her for making him think it.

"These things are very easy to disprove, Ivy," he said, but she didn't take any comfort in having read him correctly. "Even if you go to the press, I'll be vindicated very quickly. There's nothing for you to gain. We had a nice time. I'd like to remember it that way."

"They are," she agreed. "Easy to disprove." The sting of adrenaline in her system intensified as her head whirled. All she'd been thinking for three weeks was a replay of, *I have to tell him. He won't believe me. But I have to tell him...*

"And that's what you want?" he asked in a clipped voice. "For me to do a pointless paternity test? I've had a *vasectomy*," he reminded.

"So you said." It was a petty retaliation to let her skepticism hang in the air with such disdain. She added lofty, skeptical brows out of pure malice.

He snorted, and a brief flare of outrage in

his expression warned her it was unwise to provoke such a powerful man.

With a shiver of apprehension, she looked to her unpainted nails. "All I'm saying is, if you're having sex, you should be careful."

"I *am* careful," he shot back. "I always wear a condom."

"Do you?" Because after the first one had broken, they hadn't bothered using one the second time.

He swore under his breath. "You want me to believe the *one* time I had unprotected sex, my vasectomy spontaneously reversed itself and I made a baby?"

"Believe what you want. I'm telling you there's a baby inside me and there's only one man who could have put it there. But listen—" She held up her hand, striving to remember what she'd told herself when she had made her plans to seek him out. "It's obvious you had the procedure so you wouldn't become a father."

It took everything in her to speak with equanimity. In the space of a single night, he had changed her life irrevocably, and yes, on some level she felt betrayed by his assurance she had nothing to worry about. She was pregnant, overwhelmed and frightened of the future. His disbelief crushed her, but—

"I'm not here to obligate you. I felt you should know the risk you're taking with future partners. That's all." She conjured her hard-truth smile, the one that said, *I know it sucks, but this is the law of the land.*

He stood very still, sharp gaze picking her apart as though he was trying to find her ulterior motive because there was no way she could be telling the truth.

"I also want to know…" Her quavering voice trailed off. This was so hard. Her hands were so cold and numb, she nearly dropped the handbag she'd forgotten she was holding. Her heart was in her throat. "Why did you have a vasectomy?"

"My body, my choice," he threw back at her.

"It wasn't a concern about…birth defects?

Or anything medical that could affect a baby?"

His brows slammed together. "No."

She let out a shaken breath, one she'd been holding since she'd learned she was pregnant by a man who had taken a drastic step while seemingly young and fit. His reasons were his business, but a grave health concern had seemed a strong possible motive. She hadn't been able to sleep, wondering what she and her child might face.

Her knees wanted to sag as that weight of apprehension lifted. Exhaustion was catching up to her. She nodded, all of her feeling as though she more floated than stood.

"Okay. Thank you," she said faintly.

It was done. Her chest felt hollow, but tears of reaction were gathering in her throat. Definitely time to leave. She would go back to her hotel and blame pregnancy hormones for her breakdown, not her own poor judgment in getting involved with another man who was leaving her feeling used and unworthy, but at least she had done what she thought was right.

"Enjoy your party." Moving to the stairs was a walk across hot coals into an unforgiving shower of icicle daggers.

She didn't listen for him to call her back. He didn't believe her and was leaving her to raise their child alone.

It was exactly how she had expected this to go and exactly what she wanted.

CHAPTER TWO

IT WASN'T POSSIBLE. It couldn't be.

That was all Jun Li could think. He'd been in this position before, and it had turned out to be false alarms. He'd made sure after the first time that it would *never* be possible again.

But her question about birth defects and her profound relief at his answer dragged cold fingers of apprehension down the insides of his rib cage.

Jun Li didn't know one way or another if he was a carrier for anything. He'd had the procedure to ensure he would never conceive any children, healthy or otherwise.

The sound of the door opening above him snapped him out of his stasis.

"Ivy."

Calling her back was an instinctive reflex.

A man in his position developed enormous cynicism. He had learned to always be on guard against people looking for an angle to take advantage. Despite one night of intimacy, her claim was outrageous and not something his logical brain wanted to give credence to.

Even so, a barbed hook seemed caught in his flesh, one that was being tugged as though it was attached to her. He couldn't let her leave. Not yet.

Not now that he'd seen her again.

What was this disturbing reaction he had to her? He'd been warring with himself for the last two weeks, ever since his PA had told him she'd reached out, asking him to get in touch.

He'd been tempted. Very tempted. They'd had an incredible night four months ago, the kind that had burned to the ground all his previous experiences. But they wanted different things. She was moving to Vancouver, and he hated the place. There hadn't seemed any point in returning her call.

Maybe it had been arrogant to assume her call had been an attempt to rekindle their brief romance, but what other reason would there be? He'd had a quick screen for STIs, and all his results were clean.

A pregnancy hadn't occurred to him because it wasn't possible.

The silence above had gone on so long, he reached for the house phone, lifting it with the intention of asking the concierge to stop her in the lobby.

As the phone gave a beep, he heard the door click closed upstairs. She came to the rail of the loft, very pale and looking at her hands, not at him.

He could taste her defensiveness from here. It made his chest itch with premonition, the kind that warned of an approaching danger. All his sinews felt taut, as though they pulled his organs out of place.

It's not possible, he kept insisting, but there she stood, waiting for him to tell her how futile this was. He couldn't make himself say it. The knowledge that she'd been about to leave without asking him for anything was pounding in his head.

Maybe she'd realized it was a lost cause?

He never wasted words, but he was never at a loss for them, either. He didn't know what to say to her, though.

"I need to use a bathroom," she murmured.

"There's one up there."

She disappeared, and a tiny part of him relaxed at having space to think while she remained within reach.

He replaced the phone and pushed his hand through his hair, forcing himself to drink in oxygen as he tried to make sense of this.

He was normally unshockable. Even the news that Ivy had turned up here hadn't been much of a surprise. Women went to ridiculous lengths to pursue him. Not because he was some sort of player who led them on. He had been very clear to Ivy that he was only offering one night. She could have turned down his invitation to come to his room. He loved sex, but he never pressured women into it. Too many wanted the one thing he would never give them.

But he possessed a stupid amount of money and knew how to groom himself into something women found attractive. Tsai Jun Li was a catch. All the headlines said so.

He didn't wish to be caught. He had enough responsibilities without a wife and child. As such, he was judicious about when and where and with whom he had affairs.

Ivy had been a spontaneous few hours outside his normal caution. He hadn't even wanted to be in Vancouver, the city where he'd spent much of his youth, none of it happy. One of the few people he trusted had become engaged, though. Jun Li knew he wouldn't make it to Kevin's wedding, so he'd attended the engagement party and used the visit to check in on some investments and sew up a few loose threads of his old life there.

Like him, Ivy had been slipping away early. She'd emerged ahead of him, so she hadn't been trying to run into him. In fact, she'd flushed with surprised pleasure when he'd appeared.

She wasn't the most glamorous or fashion-forward woman, more fresh-faced than conventionally pretty. Her curves were subtle and her height average, but she had projected an innate confidence that appealed to him. She had amused him with her little asides.

But even before she'd asked if she could use him to get over a breakup, he'd blown off meetings and other obligations to drive her up the highway that skirted Howe Sound. He never shirked his duties. That had been the tipoff that she was dangerous to him, but they'd wound up necking in a gondola and the passion that had flared between them had emptied his head of his usual guardedness.

When they broke apart, breathless and heavy-lidded, the tone of their day had shifted. The slow-burn sensuality was a tangible entity that had imbued every word and glance. He had touched her as he drove, setting a hand on her knee and playing with her hair. She had traced patterns on the back of his hand and sent him smoky looks of anticipation.

They'd gone to his hotel for dinner, and the walk to his room afterward had felt natural. Inevitable. By then, Jun Li had told her he was leaving early the next day and wouldn't be back. Ivy confessed to recently ending a difficult relationship. She was nervous to be with someone new but wanted to move on from her ex.

He'd done his best to ensure that night was the best sex she'd ever had. If he was honest, it had been the best of his experience, too. He recalled it far too often and in far more detail than was comfortable. It had taken every ounce of discipline he had to slip away in the early hours as scheduled, the image of her naked body burned into his retinas.

He'd been tempted to stay. He'd been tempted every single day to go back to her. Tempted to turn his back on his family and duties and contracts so he could immerse himself in the pleasure she gave him.

That's why he hadn't called her back. He couldn't afford those sorts of distractions.

Now he wondered if his night with her had been a gross misjudgment. Had he involved himself with an obsessive person who chased a onetime lover around the world to make an absurd accusation? Because if she wasn't that...

His chest tightened. He'd rather think that's exactly what she was.

What did that make him, though? He hadn't stopped thinking of her and was fighting a resurgence of lust now that he'd seen her again.

Does this look like a full-term pregnancy to you?

No. It had looked like breasts straining against silk, a hint of voluptuousness across her stomach and hips. Legs that went on for miles. Oh, he'd enjoyed those legs. His groin was prickling and twitching as he recalled how her knees had hugged him. Her thighs had been hot and soft against his lips when—

Stop it.

He gave his hair another rumple as perspiration rose on his scalp. This was the reaction she was looking for—off balance and distracted by carnality.

Was she that conniving, though? Kevin wouldn't have introduced them if Ivy was an opportunist. That meant Ivy had come all this way to tell him she was pregnant, and she genuinely believed he was the father.

"It's not possible," he insisted aloud.

He would have to prove it. To himself and to her. Muttering imprecations, he called his physician.

"Failed vasectomies aren't common, but the human body can heal itself in surprising ways," the doctor said, not reassuring him at all.

Jun Li made arrangements for a test and ended the call.

In a rare fit of temper, he shouted a profanity that echoed back at him from the vaulted ceiling.

Ivy heard Jun Li release a loud, blunt curse and continued to cower in the powder room.

When he'd called her back, tears had been pressing at her eyes. She'd barely managed to face him again and had been trying to regain her composure since. Everything was catching up to her, though. One train car of emotion was piling onto another until the pressure in her chest was threatening to explode.

From the moment she'd learned she was pregnant, she'd thought only about informing Jun Li. Getting herself into a room with him had required concentration and strategy, and maybe she'd used the challenge so she could focus on that instead of the reality of being pregnant by a stranger.

It was hitting her now though. Like a wrecking ball. Her pregnancy. His doubt. The fact she was on her own when she had allowed herself the most ridiculous fantasies, ones where he greeted her warmly and claimed this was what he'd always wanted.

What a silly fool she was!

And even though she had known he would have trouble accepting what she had told him, she felt deeply scorned by his skepticism.

"Ivy." A double rap of knuckles hit the door, sending a zing of adrenaline through her. "Are you all right?"

"I'm fine." *Liar*, she accused her reflection. She was ghost-white, skin going hot and cold. She was trembling in reaction and barely able to speak because her mouth was so dry. "I'll be right out." She dabbed a wet facecloth beneath her eyes, erasing the mascara leaking from the dampness that kept gathering on her lashes.

"I'll wait for you at the door." He wanted to escort her out after all, probably to ensure she didn't sneak into any more parties uninvited.

Her sinuses pooled with unshed tears, and she tried to swallow away the lump in her throat. There was no reason to be this upset. She would be fine. Other single mothers were in far worse circumstances than she was. Once she got home and told her father, she would be able to put her life in order.

She ruthlessly pushed her emotions into a knot behind her breastbone and walked out.

Jun Li's brows came together as he looked

up from his phone and saw her. He'd thrown on a suit jacket with a silvery sheen to it, making him seem all the more armored against her.

"Jet lag is catching up to me," she said to excuse her wretched appearance, even though she'd already slept off the worst of it and had only been awake for about five hours.

His mouth tightened briefly, and his gaze raked her as though her pregnancy bump was the size of a watermelon. "Will you allow a blood draw?"

"For a paternity test?" Her heart lurched. She had thought there was a reasonable chance he might ask for one. "I signed a release form with my doctor at home."

"My doctor will do it." He opened the door. "He's on his way back to his clinic."

"At this hour?" She'd lost track but thought it must be around nine o'clock.

"This can't wait. I need to know." He was watching her closely, giving her the impression he was offering her one last chance to change her story.

She nodded agreement, and his expression grew even more remote.

They rode the elevator in silence. A car was waiting as they exited the revolving doors of the hotel lobby. The tropical night air slid across her bare arms and legs like cool silk, then the quiet of the luxury sedan closed around her as she settled into the leather seat beside him.

As it pulled away, she tried to reassure him. "Jun Li, I was serious when I said I'm not asking you to *be* a fath—"

He held up a hand. "One step at a time."

He sounded so grave, she clenched her numb hands on her handbag and let her mind empty. Gold and blue and red and purple lights flashed by. It might have been five minutes or an hour later when they were let out in front of a skyscraper. A security guard put them onto an elevator, and they were whisked up to an eerily silent foyer, where they were greeted by a man and a woman.

"Ah-Pei is our lab technician," the doctor said to Jun Li. "She'll show you where you can provide your sample." As Jun Li followed her down the hall, the doctor waved Ivy toward a lounge. "May I offer you tea?"

"I'm sorry, I thought we both had to—?" Comprehension struck. Jun Li was not providing a *blood* sample. Not yet.

Don't laugh. None of this was funny. But hysteria was ballooning outward from the emotions she was suppressing, trying to find release in one form or another, tickling and leaking between her ribs.

"Tea. Yes, please. Thank you," she accepted in a strained voice.

The doctor showed her into a comfortable lounge with a number of tea and coffee options. She kept it simple and chose a bagged herbal tea that she dropped into a cup while he started the kettle.

He chatted about his relatives in Toronto, but all Ivy could think about was Jun Li stroking himself to orgasm in another room. She recalled his shape in intimate detail. The heat and hardness against her palm. His swollen head against her tongue. The way he'd thrust with lazy purpose when he filled her and made love to her, telling her how good she felt squeezing him. The way he'd watched to ensure she was getting as much pleasure as he was. How he had waited for her to grow tense and breathless beneath him before he'd increased his speed and power so they shattered in unison...

From the depths of the corridor, she heard Ah-Pei say something that might have been, "Thank you." Was that what someone said under these circumstances?

Jun Li came into the room on a wave of energy that struck with hurricane force. The one glance Ivy dared send him noted a fading flush across his cheekbones. She went back to staring into the bottom of her cup.

"The results won't take long," the doctor said. "I'll be back shortly." He left behind a dense silence.

"There's tea," Ivy murmured, though she was only holding hers to warm her hands.

Jun Li ignored her and stood at the window,

hands in his pockets, looking so remote she wasn't sure he'd heard her.

"I'm sorry if that was difficult," she was compelled to say.

"I practice. It was easy." He bit off the words, leaving no humor in the sarcasm.

She set aside her tea and covered her face with her warmed palms, leaning her elbows onto her knees, trying to hold everything *off.* The walls were closing in anyway.

"I didn't mean for this to happen."

"Nor I. Obviously."

His subdued fury shrank her farther into herself. She had convinced herself she would feel only an air of superiority at having done the right thing by informing him, not this squirm of anguish as though she'd caused him some kind of injury. Not this sting of being blamed for something that wasn't her fault.

"All these moving parts *and* you happened to be fertile? You'll forgive me for being incredulous."

"So was I." She straightened and folded

her arms across her middle. "The signs were there right away, but you'd said it wasn't possible. I thought I was missing cycles because I was moving and interviewing for a new job." She'd been exhausted and nauseated, breasts sore, emotional. "When I finally went to the doctor, she looked at me like I was a complete idiot for not suspecting sooner."

"You're keeping it, obviously." His tone was ruthlessly neutral.

"Yes." Ivy had always wanted children. Her vision of a family had always included a loving spouse, but the fact this wasn't her perfect scenario hadn't given her any pause when she discovered she was pregnant. In fact, there was a certain relief in not having to wait until Mr. Right came along.

"Have you had any tests?" He turned to pin her with a penetrating look.

"Routine bloodwork and a scan to confirm my dates. Everything is normal. I'm not really a drinker and I take a decent multivitamin, so there doesn't seem to be any problem with my having taken so long to realize..."

She trailed off as she heard footsteps approaching.

The doctor wore an unreadable expression as he entered. He looked to Jun Li.

Jun Li nodded to indicate he should speak freely.

"You are not sterile. If you were having difficulty conceiving, we would make a more thorough study of count and motility, but the fact sperm is present and appears viable leads me to conclude your vasectomy has failed. It's possible you're responsible for this pregnancy."

Responsible. Yes. That was the avalanche of emotion befalling Jun Li to the point he could hardly breathe. It was exactly as all-encompassing as he recalled from the first time.

"Shall we move on to the paternity test?" The doctor's voice came to him from a thousand miles away.

Jun Li nodded. His heart was thrashing so hard, he could barely breathe. His head felt as if it wasn't even attached. He moved with

Ivy into a room where the technician poked them both in the arm. He barely felt it. This part was only a formality. If he could make babies, he had little doubt he was the father of Ivy's.

Condom?

What's the point?

A kick of fury with himself struck deep in his belly.

Ivy was watching him with a wary expression, perhaps anticipating some kind of blowup.

He wanted to point fingers and shout blame. He had never wanted to be in this position again. He'd taken the ultimate step to avoid it. Old betrayals and streaks of loss were fueling his anger, but he tamped all that down.

The only emotion that seeped through the cracks was guilt. Jun Li's life was one of enormous pressure and responsibility. He had never wanted to put that burden on his own child. It was a secondary reason he had made the decision not to procreate, and he'd always been comfortable with the action he'd taken.

A pregnancy had happened anyway. His baby, his *heir*, was on its way. There was no point in railing over how things were supposed to be. His energy would be far better spent working out how to fit two new people into the life he already lived.

"Paternity results will take a day or two," the doctor said as Jun Li closed his elbow over the cotton ball inside it.

He ensured the doctor had his direct number and escorted Ivy to the car.

"What hotel are you booked into?" he asked Ivy as he placed a call to his PA.

She told him, and he relayed an instruction to collect her luggage.

"What are you doing?" she blurted, cutting off a yawn she couldn't stifle. "*No.* I'm tired. I want to go to bed."

"I'm saving you the trouble of packing. You'll be more comfortable with me."

"You don't know that! My hotel is fine. I have to be up early for a cruise anyway."

"To *where*?"

"Around the harbor. I'm on a package."

Whatever astounded look was on his face made her brow crinkle defensively. "It was the cheapest way to book a flight and accommodation. It's my last chance for a vacation before the baby."

He couldn't tell if she was joking or serious. "You really think I'm going to drop you and my *unborn child* at a three-star hotel and wave goodbye?"

"I assure you the baby's current accommodation is top-notch," she said snippily. "But I'm ready for bed. If you want to talk after you get the paternity results, text me." She took out her phone and offered it for him to put in his number.

He took it and pocketed it.

"Hey!"

"You didn't come all this way to talk me into a fertility test so you could trick me into believing I'm the father of a baby that isn't mine. I believe you. We have made a baby."

"Okay. Don't you have other women to check with, though? I'd rather not hang around listening to that." She kept her hand out.

"Are you trying to make my head explode?"

"Oh, were you a virgin that night? I'm the only woman you've ever slept with?"

She was serious. For some reason it infuriated him, probably because he hadn't been able to look at another woman since her.

"That night with you is the only time I've ever skipped a condom. I don't sleep with legions of women." And he'd already done a quick mental review. Of the handful of women since his last test three years ago, one was married with a baby of the wrong age and the other two were childless. "I'm confident you're the only woman I need to worry about."

"But you *don't* have to worry about me," she insisted. "You don't even *want* children!"

"That doesn't mean I don't want this one," he shot back, tearing a small hole inside himself with the admission.

Duty required him to claim his child, but he wanted their baby in ways he couldn't articulate. It was a disturbing sensation of something in him reaching out to her, *feeling* the connection that had been forged.

"You and I are inextricably linked now." It was unsettling. He kept thinking of the way she'd tilted him off his axis once. She was doing it again, this time in a far more jarring way. "We have a life to plan."

It bothered him that he didn't know what that would look like. It bothered him that he couldn't control any of this. She had stepped back into his life and had effortlessly thrown everything into chaos. Perhaps it wasn't intentional, but that was the deeply unnerving part of it. She wasn't trying to hurt him, but he was at her mercy.

The rational side of him was reminding him to proceed with caution, to work through this methodically. Other parts were taking leaps and bounds into the future, trying to anticipate every possibility and create contingencies.

That scattered approach wasn't helpful in the long run. He knew that. He couldn't let this turn him inside out. That's why they needed a plan.

"*We* don't."

He frowned at her. "I don't remember you being argumentative."

"Gee, I wonder what got into me."

That would have been a solid gold comeback if he wasn't straining to hold on to his patience.

Tension crept into her expression as she read his mood. Her mouth tightened.

"I keep telling you I didn't come here to obligate you. *We* don't have to make a plan because *I* have one. I'm starting a new job and will live in my father's house. It's probably not *your* version of five-star—" her brow lifted with derision "—but it's cozy and in a good neighborhood with lots of young families. My father is remarrying so I'll have a stepmother and two stepsisters who already have children ready to give me lots of advice and support. You don't have to be involved at all."

He was affronted by her desire to sideline him from their child's life. From hers.

"If you didn't wish for me to be involved, you shouldn't have involved me."

"That's not fair! We each had information we needed."

"So you thought I'd book a fresh vasectomy and that would be my last thought on the matter? What kind of man do you think I am?"

"I don't know, do I? *I don't know you.*" She slouched into her seat, reminding him starkly, "But that was the deal we agreed to. One night, no strings. So yes, I expected to inform you and go home to raise this baby alone."

"The strings are there whether we want them or not. Neither of us can walk away now."

CHAPTER THREE

"THAT WASN'T WHAT we agreed," Ivy insisted, but she was so dizzy from everything that had happened she couldn't work up a stronger retort.

When she had considered all the ways this might unfold, the most likely scenario had been that Jun Li would disbelieve and reject her. Perhaps he might have taken a test at some later date to reassure himself. When he realized he could cause a pregnancy, he might have reached out for a paternity test.

In her most romantic fantasies, she had let herself dream he would welcome the news with excitement and tell her he had been thinking of her all this time, the way she had been thinking about him. But if he hadn't sought her out to continue their relationship by now, she knew it was ridiculous to imagine he had any feelings for her beyond a nice memory.

No, she had expected that once he got over the shock and got some test results, he might take some financial responsibility while they proceeded with their separate lives. He didn't want children, so why exactly did he want this one?

"Look, I'm willing to talk about you having a place in our child's life," she said tentatively. "But you understand I'm having this baby in Canada and raising it there, right?"

"No." His expression was grave. "We're marrying and raising this baby together. Here. Or Shanghai. Maybe both if the expansion is approved. We'll work that out later, but Canada is too far away."

"Exactly! That's where my life is. My family." Actually, only her father. The rest were in Hong Kong, but his decree was sending her into a tailspin. "I can't move here— Where are we going?" she asked as she realized they were crossing a bridge.

"My home."

"I said I wanted to go to my hotel. You can't *kidnap* me."

"I'm not." He gave her the annoying look men gave women that said she was over-reacting.

"Well, you're taking me somewhere against my will. What else do you call it?"

He held up a hand as his phone rang. "I have to take this."

He accepted a call while she huffed and sat back again. He told someone in Mandarin that he would not be returning to the hotel. "Ask Mutya to make the closing remarks tomorrow. Let the board know I'll be in touch in the next few days regarding the expansion." He ended the call.

"Don't let me keep you. You seem busy."

"I am. But we have a lot to work out."

"Not tonight. I'm far too tired. And now I'll have to book a car to take me all the way back…" She opened her purse before recalling, "You have my phone."

"Ivy." He took the hand she held out.

Each time he touched her, helping her in

and out of cars and elevators, he realigned the polarity in her, so she felt magnetized toward his stainless-steel core. Drawn to him.

She ought to pull away. *Don't let him take you over*, she warned herself, but her hand stayed in his while she quivered like a compass arrow.

"Did you not see the people photographing us in the lobby when we left the hotel? My staff is already fielding inquiries about who you are and why we looked so serious. It won't take any time for reporters to find you and begin pestering you. I'll take you on a day cruise if it's important to you, but everything has changed. You can't wander around anymore."

"I don't *wander*." She jerked her hand free of his, voice a jagged thing that she tried to steady. "I want to live my life. No one bothered us in Vancouver."

"Because I slipped in without my usual entourage or any publicity. I've been making headlines all week with this event. That means anyone with bills to pay will sell our image to the highest bidder along with whatever story they can make up to go with it."

"You don't know that."

"I do know that. It's happened when I've had completely innocuous lunches with female colleagues. That's why I'm careful about whom I date and how serious we get."

Her heart gave a little stumble at hearing he was discerning, even though it was more convenient to think of him as a promiscuous playboy who'd added her to his notched bedpost and forgotten her. At the same time, he was making it sound as if she would be treated like one of those poor women who dated a royal and became fair game for gossip sites.

Tears of frustration welled in her eyes. She wanted to insist on going to her hotel but was nervous now that she would be accosted. Besides, the car had arrived at a pair of gates.

"Why were you in that sky mansion if you have a house here?"

"Convenience. I took several meetings, and I don't like strangers in my personal space."

"I'm a stranger." An unwanted houseguest. A harbinger of life-changing news.

"You're family."

"I haven't agreed to marry you."

"You will."

She opened her mouth to accuse him of conceit, but he wasn't being cocky. No, his confidence was more that of a negotiator who would hammer out a deal however he had to. It was a lot harder to argue against that sort of certainty. It set a heavy rock in the pit of her stomach, because she wanted to insist there was nothing he had that she wanted while the firmness in his profile told her he would dig until he found something.

They parked, and the driver opened her door. Jun Li came around as she was straightening to her feet.

He was doing it again, standing there all effortlessly gorgeous and disconcerting, lights throwing mysterious shadows into his face. He seemed to take up all her vision and consume her thoughts. Despite her annoyance with him, she couldn't help thinking, *Now I'm here, will we sleep together?*

No.

She tamped down on her yearnings and made herself look past him so she wouldn't be so dazzled. She took in the modern architecture with its flared, pagoda-style roof over half walls dripping with greenery. Recessed lights emphasized the breezy openness of the home while creating a warm, inviting glow.

She'd always been a fan of reality shows about home makeovers and house hunting in exotic locales. Despite her misgivings about being here with him, she was intrigued.

The house was surrounded by flowering trees and twelve-foot walls disguised by vertical gardens, but who needed a backyard when there was a stunning courtyard in the middle of the home?

She goggled as she entered a high-ceilinged space where a slate pathway led between two shallow pools, one narrow and trickling with a wide waterfall that poured out of the wall, the other a much larger square pond.

"The housekeeper is off since I was planning to be in the city."

They were alone? She ignored the way her skin tightened with even more acute awareness of him.

"Your house has an island," she noted as she took in the circle of greenery in the bigger pool. It surrounded the trunk of a tree that grew toward a large rectangular hole in the roof. Posts made of warm, honey-colored wood contrasted beautifully with the tiles in the water that formed a muted mosaic of ivory and pale blue.

"This is a terrible house for a baby," she added, even though she imagined a crawler would be in heaven, paddling about in that inch of water.

"I have others."

Houses? Well, that's what she got for being rude, she supposed.

On the far side of the tree, they arrived in an open-concept kitchen of stainless steel, clean lines and bar seating.

"I can't tell if we're inside or outside," she

said as he guided her past a fireplace with a cozy lounge before it.

"This is outside." He walked her out to a backyard that was mostly water with a small strip of lawn at the base of the property's enclosure walls. The pool was for swimming, but the surface picked up the surrounding gardens and soft lights to become a reflecting pond. It was so serene, she could have cuddled into a corner on a lounger and fallen asleep right here.

"There's a dining room that way, and I use the guest room at the end as a home office." He led her up a flight of stairs.

Ivy felt as though she had climbed into the most luxurious treehouse ever built. Covered breezeways surrounded the courtyard. More greenery spilled off the ledges around her. When she went through a guest room to the balcony, she saw only a slope of trees and the boat lights on the dark sea beyond, giving the illusion they were the only house for miles.

He showed her two more guest bedrooms before waving her into the master bedroom.

"Help yourself to the jet tub if you want to relax." A huge bed dominated the center of the room, and an oval-shaped window over the sunken tub looked onto the treetop in the courtyard.

In her day job, Ivy often spoke to billionaires and powerful banking executives about wealth and investments and assets. She always told herself it was just numbers, but this was not numbers. Jun Li lived a life beyond anything she had ever conceived.

"I knew you were rich, but I thought you were... Kevin's friend," she said, shell-shocked, as she moved back into the bedroom and onto his private terrace, where he likely ate his breakfast at that teak dining table and read reports on that cozy outdoor lounge. More jungle greenery muted the noise of the outside world, and blossoms perfumed the humid air.

"Technically, Kevin is a consultant on retainer, but I consider him a friend." Jun Li joined her at the rail.

"You were the opportunity, weren't you?" she realized.

"I don't know what you mean."

"The one that made Kevin leave Hong Kong. He said a friend asked him to oversee some investments. That was you, wasn't it? That's why Kevin can afford a house in Point Grey."

Jun Li started to say something and seemed to change his mind before settling on, "My parents invested in several businesses and properties while I was schooling in Vancouver. I managed them when I lived there, but once I moved back to Shanghai and took over from my father, I needed someone I trust to look after things in Canada. Kevin wanted to return home. It was all done legally. I hope you're not suggesting—"

"No. Nothing offside, just…" She touched between her brows, starting to feel like even more of an idiot for those fantasies she'd had. "He introduced you as his former roommate."

"We did live together. In the Point Grey house," he added after a very brief hesitation. "He was commuting from Surrey. He was sleeping in his car when he had to stay late then be on campus early. I was rattling around in that big house alone."

It wasn't uncommon for parents to buy a house for their child when they were schooling overseas. Most children were lucky to get a studio condo, not a sprawling property worth millions, but that wasn't unheard-of, either.

"Since I rarely visit Vancouver and your government frowns on houses sitting empty in that market, I made the house part of his compensation package." The way Jun Li spoke as though choosing his words carefully told her there was more to the story than Kevin's lab schedule.

"But—" She'd spent way too much time remembering him naked and not enough time looking at him now. She should have already noticed the subtle details like the fact his suit was tailored to his perfect frame at a cost that had to be in the high five figures, maybe six. "I overheard some of Carla's girlfriends talking about the house being a wedding gift, the kind you don't have to return. I thought

Kevin bought it for her. You gave it to them, didn't you?"

"Again. All legal," he said crisply. "They already considered it their home, and they want to start a family."

"You gave them a *house* as a wedding gift. A Point Grey *mansion*." She couldn't help the scoff of laughter. Her voice broke with a creak of hysteria as she added, "I bought them a smoothie bullet."

"I'm sure they'll use your gift every day as well. What point am I missing?" His tone of thick boredom got her back up.

"That there's no mystery as to why you were so adamant we would only have the one night together!" Heat pressed behind her eyes. She was such an *idiot*.

"We were both leaving town," he reminded her stiffly. "You were moving back to a city I dislike. There was no point in trying to date."

"You don't like Vancouver?" Her indignation at his extreme wealth hit a wall.

"Not particularly." His mouth curled. "I have no happy memories there."

"Wow." She dropped back a step, pain emanating from her breastbone as though he'd kicked her there.

He put up a hand. "Let me rephrase that."

"Don't bother. I'm well aware you're not happy about conceiving a baby. That's certainly not going to endear you to the place! Or me. I don't care if I get swarmed by paparazzi. I'm going back to my hotel." Her blood was sizzling with a need for flight as she looked for the bag she'd absently dropped on a lounger. She snatched it up, then remembered. "Give me my phone."

"You're shivering." He waved toward the open doors back into the bedroom. "Let's go inside. Warm up."

"I'm *upset*. I have a right to be, Jun Li!"

"Because I brought you here instead of the hotel? Because I gave Kevin a house? Because you think I'm a snob who doesn't date women in a lower income bracket than my own? You asked me to be your rebound. I didn't take advantage of you," he snapped.

"You said it was okay that the condom

broke!" The words came out of her like they were pushed by fire.

His cheeks hollowed, and his nostrils flared as he drew a deep inhale.

"Let's take this inside. I have guards who patrol the grounds." He gathered her in the strength of one arm and guided her inside as though they were dancing, half lifting her so she felt as though her feet barely touched the floor.

She had forgotten he possessed such casual strength. It was unnerving to feel him so close again, surrounding her and awakening her to the feel of his touch. He'd given her such pleasure that night, but she'd been—what? Some final punctuation mark on his last night in a place he had hoped never to see again?

As they entered the bedroom, she tried to brush him off, but he was already turning away to slide the door closed behind them.

"What do you want?" he asked coolly. "An acknowledgment that I should have had myself tested more frequently? You're right. I should have. I was overconfident and you're bearing the consequence of that. Literally."

"At least *try* to sound sorry!"

Emotion flashed in his eyes, quick and searingly bright. It was as if she'd glimpsed the spark of an arc weld or the belly of an incinerator. Something that had the earth-splitting power of lightning, but was gone just as quickly, leaving outlines behind her eyelids while she blinked and his expression became a blank wall.

"Lamenting what should have been isn't going to solve what is. Sometimes life happens. *Literally.*" He mockingly repeated himself. "And we're forced to make other plans."

"I don't want to make other plans! I was finally starting the life *I* wanted." She tapped between her breasts. "Not the one I was living for some man who doesn't care about me. I landed a good job in a city I *love*—" She hurled that at him.

He only gave an impassive blink, but a muscle in his jaw pulsed, telling her he wasn't as detached as he was trying to appear.

"I was finally going to be near my dad again and I couldn't wait to—to see what other fish were in the sea." She lifted her chin. "I wasn't going to marry the next man I dated. I was going to figure out who I am without a man cluttering up my head and emotions and decisions. I was going to get a *cat*. And learn to windsurf. Now I'm *pregnant* and I can't do any of those things."

He frowned with confusion. "Why can't you get a cat?"

"That's what you heard?" She shook her head in amazement. "Women aren't supposed to clean a litterbox when they're pregnant."

"So the housekeeper will do it." He shrugged. "Problem solved."

She wanted to scream; she really did.

"Problem *not* solved. We're strangers. I'm not going to marry you when we would only wind up divorced and I'll have to take my baby home anyway."

"Our baby." His lips thinned as though he was struggling to hang onto his temper. Jun Li wasn't particularly tall, but she was on the shorter side of average and he had enough height to look down on her. "It's unlikely I will ever consent to the baby living apart from me, so remove that option from your head right now."

"You're saying that if I want to be with my child, I'm stuck with you?" She set her hand against her navel. "No. I refuse to be in a relationship with a man who doesn't love me. Not again." She had worked too hard to crawl out of that vast empty helplessness to fall back into such a void. "You don't want me, otherwise you would have called by now. Did you know I've been trying to reach you?"

The flicker of compunction in his face and the hideously rational way he said, "Ivy," tore a gasp from her throat.

"You *did*." She moved her hand to put pressure over her heart, where it felt stabbed clean through. "You didn't want to see me again. You wouldn't be speaking to me right now if I hadn't come all this way and given you this news. Would you?"

"I was informed you'd left a message." His

tone was remote. "On a geographical basis, it didn't seem like a practical relationship to pursue."

"Practical." Was that supposed to spare her feelings?

She squirmed internally, intensely hurt by his ignoring her message. He had been on her mind all this time, even before she'd learned she was pregnant. She had sworn to herself she wouldn't let her heart play tricks and see more interest and caring from a man than was really there, but when her pregnancy had been revealed, she'd been relieved. She'd had a reason to see Jun Li again. To see if they had something.

They had nothing. In fact, everything she had thought she was building for herself was also not likely to manifest.

"This isn't practical, either." She could hardly see him through the tears of injustice that were gathering in her eyes. She was embarrassed he was able to hurt her so deeply and struck the dampness off her cheeks with impatience. "I won't marry a man who doesn't want anything to do with me. I won't move to a country where I don't know a soul. You can remove *that* option from *your* head. *Right* now."

CHAPTER FOUR

WHAT WAS HE supposed to say? That he had been tempted to fly back to Vancouver, where they could screw their brains out until nothing else mattered? That one night with her had been tripping him up ever since? That he couldn't help thinking these swipes they were taking at each other tonight were the flip side of their sexual chemistry? An expression of something they were refusing to acknowledge?

"This has ceased to be productive." Jun Li moved to yank back the covers on the bed, needing to end this before it turned into something else. "You're tired and—"

"Call me emotional. *I dare you.*" Her throaty warning made him straighten and look at her. Really look at her.

Jun Li had never seen anyone as overwrought as Ivy was right now. Blotchy streaks of red had come up against her bone-white complexion. Her lips were quivering, and the rest of her was trembling like a brittle leaf in the wind. She kept trying to sniffle back tears, but they were leaking down her cheeks in frayed tracks.

If he allowed himself to acknowledge it, he would admit he was stretched to his breaking point as well. This news had rattled him to his very foundations. And because he was fighting his own existential crisis, he hadn't realized she was in the middle of one herself.

She looked as though she was facing a traumatic event. She was terrified, he realized. She was quite literally fighting for her life, and it set his heart on edge to see it.

"I believed you when you said I was protected. Do you realize that?" She spat it at him, and her bottom lip quivered.

The walls he was using to keep his own emotions at bay felt the impact of her fury. He knew that feeling of believing someone's word and learning later that trust had been misplaced. It was sickening.

"Everything inside me was going wrong. I thought I had the flu. I kept forgetting things. I was three months late and was starting to fear I would be diagnosed with something life-threatening. Because what kind of man would lie to a woman about something like that?"

The punch of accusation in her voice knocked his head back. "I didn't know."

"I didn't know that," she choked. "I sat there in that stupid paper gown and thought, *Here I am again, suckered by a man.* At some point you have to wonder, is it them or me? Was I *that* gullible? Had I slept with a man who gets his kicks running around getting women pregnant all over the world? The only way I could stomach how obtuse I'd been was to believe you didn't know." She threw that at him with a point of her finger. Then her shoulders slumped, and she seemed very small. "Which meant I had to tell you. So you wouldn't do this to anyone else. But you wouldn't even take my call. You were pre-pared to call me cab a few hours ago." She flung out an arm. "Now you're trying to force me to *marry* you? Please tell me you can hear how ludicrous you sound."

He ran his hand over his face. He wasn't impervious to the distress she was showing, but one of them had to hold on to control. If he allowed himself to fall into a tailspin like the one she was on…

No. He locked down his emotions with ruthless control.

"I'm glad you went to all this trouble to tell me, Ivy. I am." It was true. And maybe he sounded overly reasonable and patroniz-ing as he held on to this even, factual tone. It was a symptom of his determination to keep a firm grip on all this. "But it sounds as though you knew immediately that you were going to keep the baby. That's exactly how I feel. I want the baby. I want to do what's right. I'm not trying to force you into anything."

"You're trying to force me into your bed!" she cried.

"Because you're exhausted," he snapped, then reined in his temper. "We both need to take a breather while we think this through. We won't talk about this anymore tonight."

He could hear himself being more proprietary than he normally was. The buck stopped with him and he was always the final word on any decision, but he didn't shut down a discussion purely out of convenience. He typically listened and considered other points of view before closing a topic and moving on.

They were both at the end of their ropes, though. It made him do something else he normally wouldn't. No one liked to be manhandled. He knew that, but Ivy was like a punch-drunk boxer, swaying before his eyes.

He picked her up and felt her stiffen in surprise.

As he rooted his feet, bracing for a fight, she released a whimper and threw her arms around his neck. She buried her face in his throat and, with a convulsive shudder, began to sob so hard, she made his heart lurch.

It took everything he had to stay on his feet.

He had intended to put her in the bed, but he sank onto the edge of the mattress with her in his lap, all his control wavering like a house of cards in a hurricane.

He had done this to her. And well over a decade ago, he had felt exactly as sucker punched and overwhelmed as she did right now.

He adjusted her so she was under the open edges of his jacket and tried to warm her. He wasn't particularly affectionate, but instinct had him cradling her and rubbing her back, trying to offer comfort while the hard walls of his chest shook under the force of her anguish.

That old tightness, the one he'd conquered long ago, wrapped around his chest and constricted his breath. He brushed it aside and focused on calming her.

What could he say, though? She wanted him to say he was sorry, but it didn't feel like a truthful statement. He wasn't ready to examine why.

He couldn't promise her the life she had

planned out for herself, only fragments of it. Everything had changed for both of them. That was harsh reality, and he was still reeling under that fact himself.

He had to say something. She was crying uncontrollably; her shoulders were racking under the force of it. Her pained, keening noises bruised places inside him.

"We are capable, intelligent adults, Ivy. We'll find a way to make this work."

"How?" she choked out with despair.

He didn't know, but he could make nearly anything work. His degree was in economics, but he had the brain of an engineer. He could rescue billion-dollar megaprojects and work around incompetent officials from foreign governments. Once he had learned that cooking was chemical reaction and sex was biology, he'd never had a problem accomplishing either successfully.

Her lack of confidence in him was an affront, but he hadn't given her much reason to believe she could rely on him, had he?

Don't worry. I've had a vasectomy.

She must have known he would distrust her news. She had planned to have his baby without his support anyway. That humbled him.

But he was offended, too. "You really thought you had to face this alone?"

"I want to," she insisted between her sniffles. "I want to live my life, not someone else's." She must have seen the irony in clinging to him while claiming a desire for independence, because she pressed a space between them and lifted her head.

Her expression was ravaged. His arms instinctually wanted to tighten around her again. Not just for her, but for himself. The constriction in his chest had eased while he held her, but now the magnitude of what they faced loomed over them like a thousand-foot tsunami.

He ruthlessly suppressed the shadows of apprehension it cast over him. He grabbed for normalcy and shifted to set her on the mattress, then rose to remove her shoes. He set them aside, then draped the blankets across her. He would have turned out the light, but he realized she was fumbling with her dress beneath the sheets.

"Do you want a T-shirt?" He fetched one and waited while she sat up and rocked her hips to wiggle the dress free. He looped the T-shirt over her head, and she pushed her arms into the sleeves.

"Wait," she said when he started to put the dress on the chair.

She did a quick-change act, removing her bra with a release and a flick of the straps down her arms before she fished the beige satin from the neckline of the T-shirt. She handed it to him, then sank onto her back, sliding down and snuggling the covers up to her neck.

"I'm not usually like this." Her eyes were swollen, her voice rasped.

"I know." The day they'd met, there'd been a glow of optimism and conviction in her that had been exciting to witness. She'd been re-shaping her life, and the self-assurance she had projected had been the kind only this sort of hit from left field could derail. "Good night."

He leaned down and set his mouth against her own. Soft—it was supposed to be a soft kiss of comfort and good-night.

Which was a lie, he realized as the lightning strike happened, piercing into his belly and setting his blood on fire. He had wanted to see if it was still there, and it was.

Her mouth trembled under his, and her lips moved in welcome, inviting a deeper kiss. He steeled himself to give more than he took, even though he wanted to plunder her. He wanted to immerse them both in that wild excitement that hissed and sparkled behind his eyelids, promising fireworks.

He settled for holding her cheeks and caressing them with his thumbs as he rocked his mouth across hers, stealing and imprinting and lifting his head long before either of them was satisfied.

Damn, that was hard. Which was terrifying. He set his hands in the mattress beside the points of her shoulders. She would consume him if he wasn't careful. There was no avoiding that conflagration, though. Not if he was marrying her.

He had to marry her. Letting her return to Canada so he could become some sort of long-distance father was unthinkable.

At least this way… No. He wouldn't allow the lust pooling in his groin to make rationalizations for him.

He had to marry her for the sake of the baby. That's *all*.

He turned out the light.

"I can't marry someone I don't know," she said into the darkness, sounding despondent. "How are you okay with even suggesting it?"

He didn't know that much about her, either. It concerned him that someone he didn't know could affect him on so many levels— sexually enthralling him and emotionally tying him in knots. She was even destroying his basic autonomy since, married or not, his life would forever be influenced by the connection they now shared.

Even so, he let his weight settle back onto

the mattress near her hip, oddly fine with marrying someone he didn't know.

"My mother was sent to work in the country when she was seventeen. Do you know about that policy?"

"When all the students were sent to farms?"

"Yes. She was there for four years. One of her friends—she's my aunt now—talked up my father. She adores him. Most do, once they get to know him. He's the quiet sort who is always thinking. Highly intelligent and determined. My mother wrote to her parents saying he sounded smart and ambitious and kind. It was hard to move around in those days unless you had a good reason, like education or marriage. My mother wanted to return to Shanghai. My father wanted the opportunity of a bigger city. Their parents set it up, and he arrived on their wedding day. Both families were pinning their future on the marriage, but when my mother saw him, she learned he has bowed legs and a crooked spine."

Ivy drew in a sharp breath. "You said—"

"From a nutrition deficiency." He squeezed

her arm through the blankets. "It's not genetic. No one else in my family has it. My mother was upset that she hadn't been told, though. She wouldn't have asked for the marriage if she'd known, but as it turns out, he *is* smart and ambitious and kind. They're very happy, but I wouldn't be here—or here—" He waved a hand through the shadows to indicate the house. "And neither would this baby—" He nodded at her middle. "If she had known everything about him before she married him."

"That is actually a very nice bedtime story," Ivy said in a voice thick with emotion.

He had meant it as a reminder to himself that his parents had faced far more dire struggles than he ever had. They had provided him an extremely comfortable life. The least he could do was pay it forward to his own child. It would cost him hardly anything.

Just a wedding ring to a stranger.

A muted bell sounded. "Was that a door chime?" Ivy asked with surprise.

"My PA with your things." He rose. "I'll be right back."

* * *

"You look unsure," Jun Li said.

Ivy was confused. She was pregnant, but she was about to have sex with Jun Li for the first time. They were in his hotel suite in Vancouver, an extravagant set of rooms that she poked around like a wary cat, pausing to view the lights on the Lion's Gate bridge through the wide windows before coming back to set her bag near the end of the sofa.

They'd just enjoyed an unhurried dinner on a terrace. Her skin felt sensitized by all the fresh air and sunshine. Her body was loose and re-laxed thanks to a glass of wine and an excel-lent meal. When he'd invited her to his room and languidly kissed her in the elevator, she'd known this was exactly what she wanted.

"Would you rather I drive you home?" He paused in removing his jacket.

"I'm just nervous. I haven't been with any-one besides…" She was saying too much when she was trying to convince Jun Li she was intelligent and mature and self-possessed. She was trying to *be* all those things.

"You've only had one lover?" His dark brows lifted as he meandered toward her.

"How many have you had?" she challenged lightly.

Jun Li pursed his mouth. "Numbers don't matter," he decided and picked up her hand to kiss her palm. His gaze grew somber as his breath warmed her hand. "But it does make me think a night like this is a more serious undertaking for you than it is for me. Perhaps we should hit pause."

"No, I know. You're leaving first thing. I don't expect to hear from you again. It's okay if you're, um, seizing the moment." She closed one eye.

"Is that what I'm seizing?" His mouth twitched with humor.

Each time she brought that ease to his expression, she felt a thrill of triumph. "If you want to."

"Because you want to get over your ex?" He slanted a shrewd look at her. "Or get back at him?"

"Over. I'm not going to throw you in his

face. Ugh, no. I don't intend to speak to him ever again if I can help it." She revealed some of her agitation by rubbing her thumb over his knuckle. "But I was hoping to also…um… pick up a few tips on how this is done."

"Tips," he repeated with bemusement. "On seizing a moment?"

"Yes. Like do I protect my back? Lift with my legs? What's your best advice?"

He barked out a hearty chuckle at the ceiling then brought his gaze back to hers. The warmth and lingering laughter in his eyes made her heart soar.

"Ask for what you want," he suggested in a voice that managed to seduce and reassure her at the same time. "Leave if it doesn't feel right."

The fact he would say such a thing made this feel *so* right.

"I want to stay," she said firmly. "But I don't have a lot of experience. My relationship was mostly long-distance and…" She wrinkled her nose, appalled with herself that she was going to admit this, but she would never see him again. This was the magic of a one-night stand. No smirks or judgy looks to wake up to. What happened in this room stayed here. "I've never really seen the attraction in…" Hitting and quitting? "In a onetime thing. That puts all the pressure on the act itself, and I fear I'm boring in bed."

No laugh. He only tucked a stray lock of her hair behind her ear. "At no time today have I found your company boring. I can't imagine this will be any different." His gaze traced her brow and cheek and lips. "But just so I'm completely clear… What do you mean by boring? Are you saying you've never had an orgasm?"

"Only self-induced."

"Ah." His mouth twitched again at her phrasing. "I think that tells us which one of you was boring in bed. Allow me to show you all my best moves. Let's see if I can enlighten you as to the attraction."

She might have smiled or said something more, but his mouth lowered to skate across hers. It was a light question and an offer. A seal of a deal that asked if she was ready to embark.

She was. A tingle went through her from just that. All he had to do was touch his mouth to hers and she was quaking with excitement, releasing a soft moan.

A rumble of satisfaction resounded in his chest while his mouth opened across hers with more purpose, drugging her with his lack of hurry. He stroked her neck with his fingers as he slanted his head and deepened the kiss by degrees, delving and discovering and devouring her.

She could hardly breathe and set her hands on his shoulders to ground herself, then immediately splayed her fingers to take in as much of his flexing strength as she could. The nervous part of her wanted him to hurry, and she tried to drag him closer.

He turned with her, pressing her back to the wall and coming with her to press his weight into her. He wove their fingers together as he brought her hands above her head while he continued to kiss her in that lazy, thorough way.

It felt a little dirty and sexy and wicked to be pinned like this. She tested his grip, and his eyes flickered open to meet hers. His mouth lifted slightly as he checked in with her. She didn't want him to stop, though. She drew his bottom lip into her mouth and sucked, letting him know she was enjoying their play.

With a growl, his thick fingers flexed into the tender notches between hers. His hips pressed with more purpose, and he kissed her harder. Desire flared hotter, burning from her middle and licking into her erogenous zones. She quit thinking about anything except the way his deep kiss sent trickles of electric sensations to the ends of her limbs. Her breasts felt so tight they ached, but the pressure of him against her was divine. He held her at his mercy, forcing her to withstand the pleasure he was giving her.

She didn't want to be passive, though. In an instinctive move, she lifted one leg and hooked her calf against his hard buttock, dragging him even closer. He was hard behind his fly. Really hard. With a slouch of his knees and a sweep of one hand, he brushed her skirt to her waist and pressed himself against her aching mound. His open mouth sucked against her neck, and she groaned with gratification.

He released her other wrist and ran both hands all over her, making her buzzing tingles turn to bright heat and snaps of heart-skipping joy. Oh, his touch felt good. She squirmed in ecstasy while that pulsing ache in her loins intensified. She was growing damp and needy for the feel of him there.

She brought his head back and kissed him, holding the sides of his head as she blatantly thrust her tongue into his mouth. She had never had much luck being the aggressor, but he seemed to love it. He groaned and sucked on her tongue and palmed her breast. He began rocking his hips against her, inciting her desire to greater heights. The knot of arousal in her middle tightened, building with promise.

This was what the attraction was. She wanted to hurry to the good part, but she also wanted to stay like this, fondling and playing her tongue against his and savoring the streaks of need that were flooding her loins with anticipation. The build was driving her wild, doubling and redoubling, and he was with her every step of the way.

Now his hand was under the skirt of her dress, stroking her thigh, taking his time when he must know she would *die* if he didn't touch her more intimately.

"Jun Li," she pleaded, dimly aware he would drop to his knees in a moment and give her a *very* flagrant lesson in how gratifying it was to experience an orgasm that was bestowed rather than one she—

"Ivy." The world swiveled. Her eyes opened to darkness.

Her blood was screaming with arousal, her skin damp with perspiration, her body acutely stimulated.

Her hands were filled with his naked skin as he painted her against the front of his body. His chest mashed her swollen breasts through the thin layer of his cotton T-shirt.

"You're having a nightmare."

No, she wasn't. She was on the brink of orgasm. Practically having a wet dream.

"You're safe," he said, smoothing her hair.

She should have rolled away and let the dark hide her, but she was so inflamed, she stretched herself in a line against him. Her arms slid up to twine around his neck.

If she hadn't felt him stiffening inside his boxers as she moved against him, she wouldn't have opened her mouth on his throat, but she did. And she did. She licked at the soft flesh under his jaw, nibbled at the sandpapery stubble and searched for his mouth while rubbing her breasts against him.

"What—?" His voice garbled a curse as her palm swept across his chest, scraping his beaded nipple. She came back to finger and rub at that tight pebble while her leg climbed to his waist so his growing erection pressed where she was throbbing so agonizingly.

As their mouths fused and his hair sifted between her fingers, his hand clasped her buttock and he thrust against her, fully hard and steely strong. She ground her aching flesh against that thick ridge.

It took only a few pulses of pressure and friction and the libidinous intrusion of his tongue making love to her mouth. The intense golden knot deep in her belly became white hot and suddenly released streaks of joy through her whole body. She moaned, feeling herself break free.

As rolling waves of orgasmic pleasure rocked her, colored lights flashed behind her clenched eyelids. She broke their kiss to catch ragged breaths between her cries of release.

Everything in Jun Li wanted to drag away the scraps of cotton between them and thrust into her. Was she even awake?

He was. The way she'd rubbed up against him and licked his skin had got him so hard so fast it hurt. Now she was shuddering and making the most erotic noises. His heart was slamming, and his instincts were screaming at him to roll atop her and sensually devour her. He wanted to thrust deep. Claim. Bring her back to explosion and empty himself inside her.

He might have, but she moaned again, this time with tortured realization. She ducked her head and brushed at his arms, trying to roll away.

His muscles reflexively tightened before he overrode his lizard brain and released her. His senses were so heightened, he swore the scent of apricot and vanilla off her skin was pure pheromones. All he could think about was licking every inch of her.

Could she even have sex?

"What just happened?" His voice grated against his own ears, and he thought he heard her sniff in reaction.

"Nothing. A dream. Go back to sleep."

"About who?" She'd said his name, but had she been dreaming of someone else?

He reached out until he found the bumps of her spine. She was curled up like a pangolin.

"I don't want to talk about it," she said in a voice muffled by pillows and blankets. "Don't make me."

Don't make her talk? Or have sex? He wouldn't, but, "Are you okay? Is there any pain? Is the baby all right?"

"Oh my *gawd*. Yes," she hissed with another mortified noise and wriggled farther away on the mattress. "Why are you even here?"

He'd come back after an hour of imparting instructions to find her fast asleep. He'd left her case in the closet, out of the way so she wouldn't trip if she happened to rise in the night, then debated whether to crawl into bed with her.

"I wasn't planning to touch you. I wanted to be here if you woke up confused." Or tried to slip away in the night.

"Well, go sleep somewhere else. Or I will."

He should. He rarely slept with a woman, finding it disturbing. He had enough on his mind without being concerned he was flinging out an arm or snoring loud enough to wake a partner.

As he lay there debating, he heard her shaken breaths relax and even out with slumber.

Must be nice, he thought wryly. She was satisfied and he was far too aroused to drop off. He should go to another room, relieve himself of this erection and get some sleep, but he didn't want to leave her.

And therein lay the reason he should.

He didn't understand this power she had to pull him in and have him casting away his usually inviolable self-discipline.

Although was it really such a surprise when she had come apart with such abandon a few minutes ago? He gave himself a brief squeeze, both tortured and delighted to know she was still capable of such abandonment. Their night in Vancouver had been *hot*.

He relived it often, especially the part where she'd run her hands through his hair while he pleasured her with his mouth. The act always turned him on, but her response—the noises she'd made, the way she'd melted against his tongue and offered herself so unreservedly—had made him wild. When she had shattered, he'd almost lost control himself.

In the aftermath, she'd been so breathless and limp, he'd carried her to the bed like a warrior claiming spoils.

He'd had to spare a moment to dig through his luggage for a condom, though. He had an allergy, so he used nonlatex. He'd been told years before that they weren't as reliable, but he'd never had one break. The one he'd used that night had probably been expired, now he came to think of it. He hadn't bothered to check; he'd been so single-minded about getting back to her.

She'd been delightfully emboldened when he joined her, both of them hurriedly stripping each other between kisses.

"It's okay if I don't come again," she'd whispered against his mouth while they knelt on the bed, kissing and caressing. Her touch across his back while her breasts grazed his chest had made him want to close his eyes and savor the dual sensations. "I just want to feel you inside me."

"Oh, blossom. I can do better than that. This is supposed to be the best sex of your life." The play of his fingers in the dip of her lower back had made her shiver and catch her breath.

"The bar was low. This is already the best ever."

That playfulness amid the passion was unique to him. He'd found it as compelling as the rest and had thrown himself into worshipping her soft skin and pert nipples and quivering stomach, her tender thighs and the honeyed place between.

He squeezed himself again, throbbing at the memory of pressing her onto her back and rising over her. All the play had stopped then because thrusting into her had been all-encompassing. Profound.

If he'd had the discipline, he would have made love to her all night, the act of slowly pumping into her had been so intense and delectable. He wasn't superhuman, however, and it had been all he could do to wait for her.

He hadn't been so mindless that he hadn't felt the condom break when he'd picked up speed in his final strokes, though. He recalled exactly that flash of realization as it was happening. They'd both been on the verge of a powerful, mutual orgasm. It wasn't just his pleasure he would have curtailed, but hers.

He'd let desire override him and gave a last thrust that caused them both to hit their culmination. It had been spectacular. The most intense climax of his life, tearing a shout of gratification from him. The sensation of her wet heat squeezing his naked flesh had taken him to even loftier heights.

Had that moment of ecstasy been worth the consequence? He could rationalize all he wanted that he hadn't believed there could *be* any consequence. He knew his own health was good and hadn't had any concerns about Ivy's. The truth was, however, he could have pulled out and he hadn't. *He* had allowed this pregnancy to happen.

In fact, he'd damned near ensured it. A few minutes later, when he had told Ivy what had happened, she'd asked if she should visit a pharmacy.

"Don't worry. I've had a vasectomy."

"Really?"

He'd heard the curiosity in her question but had only said, "It's not something I advertise. I'd rather you kept it to yourself."

"Of course."

They'd dozed, and when she'd risen to use the bathroom a while later, he had urged, "Stay the night. I have to leave early, but order room service when you wake. Use the spa."

She did stay but didn't add anything to his bill. When she had rejoined him in bed, he'd asked if he should use another condom.

"What's the point?" she'd asked ruefully.

He'd taken that as license to go without, and this was the result.

He looked across at the shadowed shape of her beneath the covers.

There'd been so many moments when he could have made more sensible choices and hadn't. He would love to blame her for that, but it was all on him. He'd discarded his normal sense of caution and adherence to duty for sex. Really great sex, sure, but at what cost?

It added another layer to his sense of accountability. *They* had had sex, but *he* had made that baby. There was no question that he would take responsibility for both of them.

CHAPTER FIVE

IVY GRADUALLY BECAME aware of Jun Li speaking to a woman in muted tones. Dishes softly clanked. They were on the terrace, she deduced as she crept toward wakefulness. The noises were drifting in with the scent of fresh morning air, coffee and eggs.

She would love coffee, but she was settling for tea these days, usually herbal. She'd kill for a cup of orange pekoe, though.

She stretched and rolled onto her back, aware of a lingering lassitude that made waking in such a comfortable bed pure hedonism. She couldn't remember when she'd last slept so hard and woken this content. Probably the morning after—

Oh no. A ballooning horror gripped her as she recalled what had happened in the middle of the night. Please let it be a dream. *Please.*

It wasn't. She swallowed a groan of chagrin and brought her knees up as she rolled to bury her stinging face in the pillows. She wanted to die. To draw the covers over her head and stay in this bed forever.

She would have if she hadn't needed the bathroom so pressingly.

With a whimper, she lifted her head to ensure no one was around. Damn him, Jun Li had thoughtfully left a silk robe with a cherry blossom print on the foot of the bed.

She snagged it on her way to the bathroom. Why, why, *why* had she thrown herself at him like that? She'd practically attacked him!

In the bathroom, a brand-new toothbrush sat beside the sink along with geranium-scented shampoo, conditioner and body wash.

Ivy used the toothbrush then took the rest into the shower, mostly to put off seeing him. The warm rain from the sunflower head washed the dullness from her brain but none of the ignominy from her conscience. After drying off, she combed out her wet hair and moisturized every inch of her body with a luxurious green tea and lemongrass–scented lotion until she had run out of excuses to avoid him.

Also, she was starving.

Which didn't mean joining him on the terrace was easy. No, it might only be three steps to the table, but it was a mile-long walk of shame.

"Good morning." He wasn't openly smug, but he watched her with a morning-after acknowledgment of intimacy that he hadn't hung around long enough in Vancouver to let her witness.

"Thank you for this," she murmured of the robe, hyperaware that she was naked beneath it.

"More clothes are being delivered. I wanted to let you sleep, but I didn't want you to have to come looking for me amid the crowd."

Crowd? "I have clothes. Don't I? I thought my luggage arrived last night."

"Your things are in the closet, but you'll need a full wardrobe. Twice, I'm told, since maternity wear is its own thing." His attention swept down to where the lapels of the robe exposed her upper chest. "I've been reading about how a woman's body changes during pregnancy. It's remarkable."

Still worried that her orgasm had harmed the baby?

"I packed maternity wear. I didn't wear my dress last night because it kind of gave the game away."

She accepted the plate he uncovered. It held peeled and halved boiled eggs with grilled avocado, cherry tomatoes, a bowl of tropical fruit, a side of subtly spiced noodles and a small banana. She would never get through it all, but she was hungry enough to give it a shot.

"You'll need more than one dress. The delivery is all ready-to-wear, but my mother is looking forward to introducing you to some of her favorite designers."

"You told your mother about the baby?" She nearly bobbled the plate and set it down with a clack. "I was going to tell my father when I got home. She won't post it online, will she?"

"No. I was going to do that as soon as I asked you if there was anyone you needed to notify first. We'll call your father after breakfast." He glanced at his watch. "Before it gets too late there. Is he well? Can he travel within the week?"

"To where?" Her nerveless fingers lost control over her chopsticks and sent a cherry tomato rolling.

"Shanghai." He neatly caught it as it fell off the table. "For our wedding." He popped it into his mouth and chewed. "Next Friday."

"I told you I won't marry you!" Last night began to seem like an even bigger mistake than it obviously was. Had he read it as some sort of capitulation?

"Marriage is the most practical solution."

"For *you.*"

He had started to pick up his coffee but set it down again. "I had hoped once you slept on it, you'd see the advantages to you as well."

The way his gaze flashed into hers said, *I remember everything.*

The great big lumbering elephant she'd been trying to ignore was suddenly tapping her shoulder with its trunk.

Ivy blushed. Hard.

"Just to be clear, I will never see my child as something that should provide me advantages. Certainly not material ones like a wealthy husband. Marrying up has never been a goal of mine. I won't use my baby to do it."

"I thought when couples fought over money, it was because there wasn't enough. If I were middle-class, would you accept? Are you suggesting I divest of a few zeroes to earn your hand?"

"I'm saying you wouldn't be asking for my hand if I wasn't pregnant." She pinched a bite of mango and ate it.

"I wasn't going to marry anyone. Don't take it personally."

She snorted. "It feels personal when you're asking me to marry you and I know it's the last thing you want. At least tell me why you were avoiding it."

"It simply isn't—wasn't—" he corrected "—something I wanted for myself. I'm already responsible for hundreds of projects, thousands of jobs and billions of dollars. I respect how hard my parents worked to build what I manage today, but I never wanted to put this much responsibility onto my own child. I…" His cheek ticked, and he stole a moment to sip his coffee before admitting, "I had a scare with a fellow student my last year of high school."

"You got someone pregnant?"

His fingertip tapped his cup before he said flatly, "No. But for a short while I believed I had."

Ivy stopped eating and watched his gaze focus on the skies over a distant horizon.

"A fellow student?"

"Yes. My first relationship. First time living alone. I wasn't nearly mature enough to become a father. When she told me, I was terrified. I called home to tell my parents but didn't get a chance. My father's health had taken a downturn. The semester was almost finished, so I said I'd be home soon within a couple of weeks, but I didn't know what I was going to do."

"Was it a false alarm?"

"No. She was pregnant, but it wasn't mine. When I asked her to come to China with me to meet my parents, she confessed there was another man in the picture. He was her manager at the fast food place where she worked after school. He was a few years older, engaged to another woman. He had told her to pretend it was mine because he didn't want it, and look at all the money I had. It was such a mess." He used a light tone that dismissed the whole thing as the hijinks of youth.

Ivy wanted to take his hand and say *Don't do that.* "It was your first love. You must have been crushed."

His face hardened beneath the stubbornly impassive expression he was maintaining. "The not knowing whether it was mine was torture. Lucky me, I had the kind of money to pay for a high-quality paternity test. When we learned I wasn't the father, she went away to stay with relatives."

"Why do I get the feeling you're still wondering if you should have married her anyway?" she asked gently, but with a pang behind her breastbone for the intense young man he must have been.

"She cheated and that's hard to forgive, but she was a child, same as me. That other guy was old enough to know better," he muttered.

"He was her boss."

"That too." His lip curled in disgust. He sat up straighter, giving a small shrug as if divesting himself of the past. "The whole thing left me furious and disillusioned. I had been prepared to cut my education short to become a husband and father. I felt manipulated and realized what a target I had become because of our wealth. How vulnerable I would be if I had a child."

Those sobering words made her hear again *You can't wander. I have guards.* Was that why he was so adamant they marry? He was worried about them?

"My father was still ill, and I was facing the formidable task of taking over from him sooner or later. Of course, my parents have always expected me to marry and have a child someday, but I couldn't see a time when I would be prepared to take on a family when I had so much to shoulder as it was. I couldn't see wanting to put that burden onto my own flesh and blood. When I got to university, I had a student doctor perform the procedure."

She quirked a brow. "I have to ask. Are you sure it was done correctly?"

"Fair," he snorted. "Given my age, he used a technique that was supposed to be reversible, but I did the tests afterward. Every year, for the first while. I only fell down on it the last few years because I've been busy with work and thought... Well, we've seen what happens when we get complacent, haven't we?"

"I'm still surprised." By all of it. "I'm shocked

you believed me enough to get tested, given you went through all that."

"You were too upset not to take you seriously," he said soberly. "And I had to know. Please don't mention any of this to my parents, though. I never told them about the scare."

"Of course not. How long had you been in Canada when it happened? You said it was your first time living alone." Had he been sowing the wild oats of a young man away from home for the first time?

"Six, almost seven years."

"Oh. Wow. Most of the foreign students I know didn't come over until they were fifteen or sixteen. You were *ten*?"

"Eleven. When the opportunity came up to send me to Canada, my parents jumped on it. They could barely afford the payments, but they didn't know how long the window would be open. It began as a way for me to learn English, but as their fortunes grew, I was able to help with their early investments there."

"Like Kevin's house?"

"Exactly. Many eggs, many baskets, has always been my father's philosophy. And my time there allowed me to take advantage of a fast track to permanent residency."

So much for dangling that as an incentive to live with her in Canada.

"But you weren't happy there," she recalled from last night.

"No." He dropped his gaze, giving her the impression he was not telling her the whole truth when he said, "I was young to be sent around the world away from my parents. I thought it would be an adventure, but the culture shock was enormous." His cheek ticked as though he was revisiting a difficult memory. "After I was getting As in English, I could have told them I didn't want to go, but I knew how hard they had worked to give me that advantage. My father is in pain every day of his life. My mother spent years away from her own family. Surely I could handle a bit of rain and birthday parties without my cousins if it meant I could provide all of us more options later."

"You were homesick," she realized.

"It lessened over time, but…" He shrugged it off. "I knew Canada would never be my home, so I didn't allow it to feel like one. It was a place where I worked, preparing myself to take over from my father. The day you and I spent together was probably the most carefree I have ever been in that city. I still feel a dereliction of duty over it."

"I can't tell if that's a compliment or a complaint."

"It's a concern. I can't bring myself to complain." His gaze heated, and she blushed.

Last night's passion was suddenly here between them again, but the housekeeper appeared with freshly squeezed juice for Ivy and an apology that she directed at Jun Li.

"Your assistant asks if you have read his text? He says it's urgent."

Jun Li made a face and picked up the buzzing phone he'd been ignoring. He tapped the screen, read, then said, "Hmm. Your father is receiving inquiries from the press. When you didn't answer his calls or texts, he tried to reach you at the hotel. He was told you checked out, but you haven't notified him where you've gone, so he has threatened the hotel manager with a call to the Canadian Embassy if he doesn't hear from you soon." He withdrew Ivy's phone from his shirt pocket. "My bad. I turned it off so it wouldn't wake you."

Ivy stared at her phone as if he was pointing a loaded weapon at her.

"What am I supposed to tell him?"

Jun Li suggested she get dressed first and took her to see the clothes he'd had delivered to the basement.

Ivy came down the stairs to a big, comfortable lounge with an overstuffed sectional that faced a big screen. A wet bar was tucked into a corner on the far side of a pool table.

The top half of one wall was glass that looked onto the bottom of the pool, allowing the sunshine beaming into the water to bounce in and leave patterns on the floor. When she washed her hands at the sink in the powder room, instead of seeing herself in a mirror, she could wave at whoever was swimming.

A child would find that infinitely amusing—and probably wash their hands more often, Ivy thought wryly.

This home was actually a work of art, and she was falling in love with it by the second.

She glanced into a fully stocked gym on her way to the other spare bedroom, which had been filled with racks of clothes. Jun Li was already sifting through the selection.

Ivy normally hated salespeople trying to guess what she might like. It felt especially strange to have Jun Li hold things up to her and replace them on the rack before she could decide one way or another.

"Do you want me to look a certain way?" she asked with indignation.

"No," he said with absent surprise. "Pick whatever you like. I just like shopping. It's my vice. In high school, I didn't go to parties. If I wanted to be around people, I went to the mall."

She wondered if that was why he had insisted they browse the gondola gift shop when they'd been enjoying their stolen day in Vancouver. He had bought her a crystal sun catcher and made a remark about her needing luck to catch any sun if she was moving to Vancouver, but he'd offered it as a housewarming gift anyway.

She had thanked him with a kiss that she still remembered as passionate enough to curl her toes. She had planned to put his gift in the baby's room.

"Try this," he coaxed, snapping her out of her reverie.

It was a flapperesque drop-waisted sleeveless dress with a sailor collar.

"I usually wear clothes that are more classic and conservative." But she was almost always looking for something that could double as work wear, nothing that was purely for the pleasure of looking cute.

She tried it and, as she smoothed the dress down her hips, instantly felt more comfortable in this changing figure of hers.

"It suits you." The admiration in Jun Li's

gaze made her even more conscious of her body. Of the fact she was bustier and had hips and he seemed to think that suited her, too.

Their gazes tangled. The way his gaze dropped to her mouth made her lips part and her breath stutter.

In the dark of his bed, he'd kissed her as though starving for her. His whole body had been taut against hers, his fingers digging into her buttocks as he rocked her world.

She watched the temptation fog his gaze. Her skin tightened. She licked her lips, anticipating the feel of his mouth crushing the tingles from her own.

If he had kissed her right then, demonstrating that he couldn't resist her any more than she could resist him, it would have gone a long way to reassuring her that she hadn't made a complete fool of herself last night.

But just as his hand came up and he looked ready to cup the side of her neck and kiss the daylights out of her, he stepped back and dropped his hand to his side.

"Almeida. Come in. Ivy, this is your stylist. I'll wait upstairs." He disappeared.

Almeida smiled knowingly as she touched a flat iron to Ivy's hair and gave her a few swipes of makeup. Ivy tried to quell a blush that was both unrequited lust and anguished embarrassment that she couldn't hide how she was reacting.

She came back upstairs to find Jun Li holding a meeting with a half dozen faces at the dining room table. He introduced her to everyone. One was his PA from last night, and another was a public relations person who came outside with them and photographed them sitting side by side on a wicker love seat with the lush garden wall as a backdrop.

"I thought we were calling Dad? Why is this happening?" she asked through a gritted-teeth smile.

"For the announcement."

She snapped her head around. "I haven't agreed to anything."

"Not yet," he allowed. "But when you do, the photographs will be ready."

He was back to railroading her. Why? Because he'd seen how weak she was when he had almost kissed her? Or because of the way she'd behaved in the middle of the night?

Her hand curled into a fist beneath his. "You're taking things for granted. Last night didn't mean what you think it did."

He lifted his hand from hers and jerked his head at the photographer. "Leave us."

The photographer scurried away, and Ivy sat there with her face on fire, her flush stoked by fury and hurt and humiliation. A silence pulsed between them.

She could tell he was looking at her, but she refused to look at him. She stared into the stillness of the water.

"What exactly do you think I'm taking for granted?" he asked dangerously.

"That I'm going to marry you just because I—" She couldn't say it. She had to clear a thickness from her throat in order to speak at all. "Last night was just…hormones." She flicked a glance to ensure there weren't any housekeepers or any of the other staff lurking and overhearing. This was humiliating enough. "It's like I have an amplifier inside me. When I'm tired, I'm exhausted. When I'm hungry, I'm famished. I'm trying really hard to be rational over how things are going between us, but I'm fighting tears every second along with an urge to scream. That's how pregnancy affects me. I'm emoting for two. You could have been anyone last night." That was a blatant lie, but it felt like the only way she could save any face.

"Is that right?" He released a jagged, humorless laugh and set his arm behind her on the back of the love seat so he was angled toward her. He touched her chin, urging her to look at him. "Because if you're telling me that pregnancy has made you so amorous you'll wake a man up for sex and come apart before you're even naked, you'd better believe I'm going to be the man in bed beside you."

Her heart hitched and she wanted to pull away, but their stares were locked again, and his thumb was playing across her bottom lip, making it feel swollen and buzzing.

She saw the hungry wolf in him rising, but his nostrils flared, and his expression hardened.

"We'll save it for our wedding night, though. Incentive," he added in a drawl.

Again, she was struck by how easily he could take or leave her while she was ready to fall into his arms. She forced herself to drag forth her own dry chuckle.

"I won't marry you for your money. You think I'm going to marry you for *that*? Good luck."

His hand came back to the side of her face and his head swooped down. His mouth crashed over hers, not painfully, but devastating all the same. His lips swept untamed over hers again and again, exploding her world. He erased her mind of everything but him, exactly as he had from the first time he'd kissed her when they'd stood on a platform three thousand feet in the air.

Her response had nothing to do with her

pregnancy. He built her up and tore her down and remade her in a matter of heartbeats. Made her his. Again. Still. Because she'd been his since the first time he'd raked his lips so tenderly across hers, whether she wanted to give herself to him or not.

As he drew away, she realized her hand was clenched around the strength of his wrist. Her lips clung to his, and her eyes felt too heavy to open. Breathing was something other people did because they didn't know how wonderful it was to be smothered by his mouth.

A final touch of his lips to hers that was almost a peck of comfort. His voice was a rumble of masculine strength and suppressed desire.

"Yes, blossom, I do think you'll marry for that."

A wounded gasp left her before she could catch it back. His profile tightened slightly. Compunction? Something else that she couldn't read because she was so angry, her eyes were blurring with unshed tears.

"Because *I* will," he admitted in such a

stark, impactful voice he nearly knocked her into the pool with it. "So let's call your father and tell him our happy news."

CHAPTER SIX

THEY CALLED HER father from Jun Li's office, a sparsely furnished space with teak floors and a New Age desk that looked like the metal had poured off the one side to create its own support. A wall of locked glass protected some discreet filing cabinets along with rare books and a few small and likely priceless sculptures.

Despite what he'd said by the pool, Jun Li didn't force the issue in front of her father. He sat beside her and let her do most of the talking.

Her father's eyes welled with happiness at the baby news, and Ivy said she and Jun Li were still discussing how they would proceed. She promised to call him back soon.

As she set the phone aside, she couldn't face the questions in Jun Li's expression. She walked out to the pool, where she kicked off her slippers. She plopped down on the edge to dangle her feet in the water, trying to re-calibrate. Trying to think.

But think about what? She knew what Jun Li expected her to do. She knew what her father expected. She knew what the whole world would expect once it was revealed she was carrying Tsai Jun Li's baby. She knew what she would expect of herself if this was a hypothetical situation posed as a parlor game.

Reality was far more complex and arduous.

She was so deep in thought, she only distantly heard Jun Li say, "Do you see anything you like?"

His question didn't make sense. A shadow unexpectedly descended in front of her face. It startled her so badly, she reflexively struck at whatever it was, sending it flying into the pool.

Sparkling droplets flashed as they scattered and rained into the water with soft plinks. Something square and flat landed on the surface and sat there like a boat that was taking on water.

"Apparently not." Jun Li straightened and peeled his shirt up and off, blinding her with his tawny, muscled chest and small dark nipples and abs that were so perfectly defined, they were like stacked blocks of store-bought masculinity.

"What was that?"

"Rings." He opened his belt and peeled himself down to his boxer briefs, stepping out of his slippers.

"Like...diamonds?" She looked with horror into the settling water to see glints of ice and gold sitting on the bottom of the pool. "Why would you stick them in my face like that?"

"Why would you throw them in the pool?" He took a breath and dived in without waiting for her answer. As he skimmed the bottom, his hands swept out a few times before he surfaced to grab the sinking tray.

He swam over to set the tray beside her. It still had a couple of rings stuck into its velvet slots. He poured several more into her hand.

"Is the jeweler still here? What if we don't find them all?" She was so embarrassed.

"Are *we* looking for them?"

"Yes, I'm the spotter. You missed one over there." She pointed to a shimmer of dark green.

He took another breath and made a second tour of the pool's floor while she quietly goggled at the rings she was handling. The man certainly wasn't afraid to be generous. All the stones looked to be at least three or four carats, not that she knew much about such things. There weren't just diamonds, either. There were rubies and emeralds and sapphires. Their shapes ranged from round to square, heart-shaped to marquise, princess to pear. Many were haloed in smaller sparklers that also coated the platinum bands. All were as tasteful as they were extravagant.

Two more trips and she said, "That's all the pockets filled. Should be all of them."

"Good." He hooked his elbow on the ledge beside her thigh. "I'll ask again. Do you see anything you like? We can get something made if you prefer. You don't have to, you know, *throw them away*."

"I love how you act so accommodating while expecting me to do exactly what you want." She pushed the tray back from the edge of the pool and tucked her palms together between her knees, scowling across the pool.

"Tell me what you think we should do, then. I'm all ears."

She didn't have any idea and he damned well knew it. His story this morning about living away from his parents for so many years had gotten to her. If she hadn't had such a close relationship to her father when her mother had passed, she didn't know how she would have survived.

Then there was the part where the sexual attraction between them seemed to be strong as ever.

I do think you'll marry for that. Because I will.

She heaved an angry sigh. "Wanting to have sex with me and wanting to have a relationship with me are two different things. You didn't call me back. You don't want *me*. It's very hard to commit my life to that."

In the most obscenely effortless show of athletic strength and grace, he levered himself out of the pool and sat next to her in a swoosh of dripping water and gleaming, golden skin.

She swallowed and averted her eyes. "Don't use sex to get your way," she warned. "It's beneath you."

"That's up for debate," he said under his breath, bracing his hands on the ledge next to his splayed thighs. "Tell me about the man you were trying to forget when we made our baby."

"What? No. Why?"

"Because you're comparing me to him. I want to know if it's a fair assessment."

"I'm comparing the situation. You're nothing like him." For starters, sex with Jun Li nearly knocked her off the bed. With Bryant, it had been a lot of fumbling and her trying to be sexy and set a mood and winding up feeling as though she was faking the whole thing.

"He was your only lover besides me. Do I recall that correctly? There's been no one since, if I was the only contender for paternity. What was his name?"

"Our previous relationships don't matter. You said so," she reminded him.

He kept his hard stare pinned on her, refusing to let her dodge or dissemble.

"Bryant," she admitted in a mumble.

"You met at university?"

"High school. He was going into environmental science. I admired his principles."

"Remind me to show you my wind farms."

She rolled her eyes then dropped her gaze to the egg-beater swish of her feet in the water.

"He knew my mother," she admitted. "Kind of. She was his orthodontist. And mine." She automatically showed her teeth since telling people that detail about her mother always prompted a demand she prove it by showing off her perfect smile. "I liked being with someone who had a memory of her, even if it was only that."

"I presumed you'd lost her since you only spoke about your father and said he's remarrying. I'm sorry."

"Thanks. I was sixteen. She was only forty-four. Struck by a car on a crosswalk on a rainy night."

Ivy had thought she had learned to live with her grief until her breakup with Bryant had been all the harder for not having her mother's shoulder to cry on. Then she had wished she could tell her about the surreal day she'd spent with Jun Li. Now she had a pregnancy she couldn't share, and soon there would be a small face with traces of her mother in it. She was missing her more than ever.

"What happened to cause your breakup?" Jun Li's attention sat like a weight on her. She sensed him holding very still as though gripped by a tension he didn't want to reveal.

"Nothing," she said ironically. "Many acts of nothing. Have you ever heard the expression that you only understand your life in reverse? When I look back, I see all the times where I should have cut and run, but at the time I had a vision of where we'd end up so I stuck it out, patiently waiting for that magical day to happen."

"What kind of magic?"

"Marriage. Once we lost Mom, all I wanted was a family that was intact again. I felt like I couldn't be happy again until I had that. It doesn't make sense when I say it out loud, but it's how I felt."

"He didn't want that?"

"No, but I didn't see it. I thought other things were in our way, like education. We were pursuing different programs, so we went to different universities. We actually broke up, but neither of us saw anyone else, and we were always texting and calling. Pretty soon we were flying out to see one another. Except, when I look back, I see that he came to Vancouver to see his family. I was an afterthought." A booty call.

"I expected to start our life together once we got our degrees, but a professor persuaded me to try for an opportunity in Hong Kong. Bryant said I should go for it because he wanted to get his master's and would be away doing field research. Since I was working and he was still in school, I sent him money for things like textbooks and..." She felt like such an idiot. "In my mind, we were making sacrifices up front to ensure we had good careers ahead of us. We were building a strong foundation for our combined future."

"Was he cheating on you?"

"I don't want to sound even more naive than I already was, but I genuinely don't think so. He borders on obsessive about his research. It's fair to say he had a mistress in that regard." She quirked her mouth, dismissing how many hours of editorial work she'd put into his papers. How many times she had double- and triple-checked his data sets. "And I don't think he was consciously using me. He's just a self-involved person. I was a comfortable partner, out of the way, but available when he needed a sounding board or a cheerleader."

She skipped over the part where Bryant had made endless excuses and canceled his trips to come see her in Hong Kong. How she couldn't even count on him to call when he said he would. She was embarrassed by the way she'd clung to a vision that simply hadn't existed.

"I thought it was the nature of commitment that sometimes you have bad times, and you have to stick it out until the better times come around. Then I tried to make the better times happen by taking a transfer to Toronto. It was actually a demotion, but I wanted to be with him. I wanted to start our life together."

"He let you transfer before he told you that it wasn't going to happen? What a jerk."

"He was going away and needed someone to pay the bills for a couple of months, so yeah, that's what he did. When he got back, I finally asked him point-blank if we were ever going to marry. He said he didn't see it happening, so I moved out and started interviewing in Vancouver. I called Kevin while I was visiting Dad, thinking he might have some leads. He invited me to the party, I met you and now we're here."

Bryant's rejection had been four months old when she had met Jun Li. It still felt fresh. She still held deep doubts in her appeal as a woman. In her ability to see what was real in a relationship. In the wisdom of trusting a man to have her best interests at heart.

"How is that situation similar to ours?" Jun Li asked with quiet challenge. "I want to marry you. I want to support you and keep our family intact."

"You want me to arrange my life around yours. For your convenience. You don't know me. You don't want *me*." She set the side of her hand against her breastbone, feeling the knife of that truth deep in her heart.

"You could have had this baby alone and never told me. You didn't."

"Because—"

"Because you were doing what you thought was right for all of us," he said over her. "Which makes you a woman with integrity. If I'm going to marry, surely that's a quality

I should want in a wife? You're also intelligent and funny and self-sufficient. I'm sorry that other man made you feel undervalued. I won't do that."

His promise shook things in her. Made cracks and fissures open up for hope to leak out and begin to drug her into believing this would work.

"I won't know if that's true until eight years have passed, though. Will I?" And then, because his sincerity was making emotion gather in her throat and well in her eyes, she waved at her face and said, "See? Everything is exaggerated."

"Including your fears?" he asked gently, cupping her cheek and using his thumb to catch a tear and whisk it away before it rolled down her cheek.

She sniffled, admitting, "Maybe."

He turned away, hesitated, then said, "Incoming," as he presented the tray again.

"Tsk." She looked away, refusing to let him see he was making her smile as he offered the soggy tray of rings. When she looked down at them, the refraction of rainbows dazzled her. "These just make me realize how different we are."

"I'm not trying to buy you, Ivy. I'm saying this is the life our baby is entitled to. That's not a criticism of the life you can offer, but I can offer more. Can we agree that we both want to give our child every possible advantage?"

That was not what he was asking her to agree to. He was asking her to marry a stranger, one who had already upended her life. Now he wanted her to believe he was offering everything she longed for in one go.

Did he realize she wanted a husband who loved her?

Maybe in time they would fall in love, a little voice said inside her.

Oh, Ivy, don't do that to yourself again!

She had a baby to think of, though. A baby entitled to...*this*. A baby entitled to form relationships with both its parents. Jun Li was a man worth knowing, wasn't he? Smart and ambitious. Certainly not *un*kind.

I'm sorry that other man made you feel undervalued. I won't do that.

"This one is by a Vancouver designer." He drew out a true-blue diamond in a triangular cut. It was surrounded by white diamonds that poured down the split band in a swishy curve. "Inspired by the snowy mountains on Vancouver's North Shore, or so I was told. Perhaps it would help you feel less homesick?"

Eight years with a man she had believed she loved, and he had never once said anything so thoughtful or personal. Or offered a ring.

Before she realized what she was doing, she lifted her hand to see if it fit.

It did. Perfectly. If it had been red, it would have matched the fire that spontaneously ignited in her heart, surrounded by an incandescent glow of hope.

"You'll marry me?"

She made herself look beyond the giddy euphoria of sitting in paradise wearing a priceless piece of art on her finger while a gorgeous, sexy man asked her to spend her life with him.

There was no real debate, though. She had made the choice the moment she'd realized she was pregnant. Her first thought had been that she would have to tell him, and there'd been all those underlying yearnings. *Let him want this baby as much as I do. Let him want us.*

She had been confident she could raise the baby alone, but she didn't want to. She wanted her baby to know its father. *She* wanted to know him.

And there was something bigger at play, too. She didn't believe in destiny in the way of a god preordaining a meeting of souls, but this baby had come about through ridiculously impossible odds. That had to mean her life was supposed to entwine with Jun Li's, didn't it? Was there any sense in resisting the inevitable?

"I will." Her voice was barely a whisper, overwhelmed by the scope and gravity of her promise.

"Good." He gathered her into his lap and kissed her. Once to seal the deal, then a little longer, until the spark of last night's passion began to flare between them. He hardened against her bottom, and she curled her arm around his neck.

She felt his muscles gather. He was going to rise and carry her into his office to—

He leaped into the pool with her in his arms.

As they plunged into the water, her scream of outrage was caught by his laughing mouth.

CHAPTER SEVEN

JUN LI HAD GOTTEN what he wanted. They were getting married in ten days.

He ought to be pleased. He *was* pleased, but his thoughts were racing with everything that needed to be done. He had worked out in the gym first thing, trying to exercise this restless agitation in him, but his muscles were still tense and he hadn't outrun the nameless thing chasing him.

It had a name, he reminded himself scathingly. He just didn't want to acknowledge it.

He wanted to call it sexual frustration because Ivy had gone to bed before him and he'd made himself sleep elsewhere. He'd woken early and hard, thoughts swirling with how her sexual responses were "amplified."

He ached for her, had done for months. It was all the more acute now that she was under his roof, but he had gone without sex before and hadn't suffered this sensation of dogs snapping at his heels.

He knew what the real problem was, but he wanted to be strong and capable and reliable. Fully in control of everything around him and within him. Admitting he was prone to depression when things got too big for him to handle was demoralizing. This shouldn't be too big. Ivy was doing the real work. All he had to do was keep her warm, dry and fed.

He'd been fine for years without medication. He resented even having to think about taking it again, but of course this massive life change had the power to knock him off balance. He was as prone to self-delusion as anyone else, but he wasn't stupid. This was the sort of thing that *should* make a man pause and take stock. That's what his body was telling him.

Easier said than done, and he would cut out his own tongue before he said aloud to Ivy that the prospect of marrying and having a child was threatening to depress him.

He glanced across at her. Apparently, he'd turned into one of those lechers who couldn't take his eyes off a woman's chest, because he noted *again* the way her top showcased her cleavage. That baby really was amplifying everything.

But they'd had a spat on the flight from Singapore and he wasn't sure if she was speaking to him yet. He'd been busy taking calls and organizing things and said, "My mother needs a guest list from you as soon as possible."

"For the banquet? It's just my father's fiancée and her daughters. The names I gave you."

They had agreed the ceremony would be an intimate civil affair with only their parents in attendance, but the banquet would be more lavish.

"What about friends? What about your family in Hong Kong? No one wants to come?"

"Well, of course they'd love to come, but they can't drop everything and book a flight to China at a moment's notice. For a weekend. It's something they have to save for." She gave him a look that called him a wealthy, out-of-touch knot head. "They'll visit me later, after the baby comes."

"They don't have to save. My travel office will make all their arrangements. I have a block of rooms set aside at the hotel. Once they're on the list, you only need to give them the link. They'll have three nights with all their meals and travel covered. Invite as many people as you want."

She snorted. "That's very generous, but I'm not going to hand out an all-expenses-paid trip to everyone I know. How many people are *you* inviting?"

"Mother's list has three hundred."

Ivy had glared at him for a full minute before she had pulled out a small tablet and plugged in some earbuds to shut him out while she, presumably, curated a list of her closest two or three hundred friends and family.

"Are you feeling all right?" Jun Li asked. "You've been quiet." Still angry?

She drew in a breath and sat straighter, seeming to become aware they were in the car winding through a neighborhood in Quinpu District.

"Just thinking. There's a lot to process."

"The wedding?" he guessed.

"Yes. I don't know what I expected, but…" She sighed and waved it off. "Turning down that job bothers me more. I would have had to take maternity leave in a few months anyway, and I haven't really burned a bridge. I'll always be able to find work if I want it. Executive recruiters are still sending me leads," she said with a flick of her hand to where her phone was tucked into her handbag. "I have savings. But it bothers me that I won't have an income. It feels very retro to become dependent on my husband."

She was reluctant to let a man govern her life again. He understood that and had a small desire to punch her old boyfriend in the throat for treating her so poorly, since it left her with very little faith in him.

"I'll hire you when you're ready to work again," he promised.

"I don't want a job by nepotism."

"You just said headhunters are still after you. That suggests you have qualifications that would benefit my organization."

"I guess." Her mouth crinkled in a reluctant smile. She turned her attention out the window as the car slowed at a pair of gates. "This is where my family will stay?"

"If you approve, yes." He scratched his upper lip. She was going to be mad again, but he would wait until she had seen inside before starting that fight.

Many of the houses in this area were Western-style mansions, but this one was very modern and sleek, almost looking as though colored children's blocks had been assembled in a haphazard but pleasing way. A staff of eight greeted them as they entered.

The butler introduced each one, adding to Ivy, "Once your guests arrive, we'll have four more."

"Oh. Um, I'm sure my family will be very comfortable. Thank you."

They dispersed, and Jun Li watched her as she moved from the spacious foyer to an airy lounge. It was decorated in a tasteful and elegant color palette of soothing grays with gentle pops of dusty blue and muted gold. The wall was a unique half circle that showcased as much of the serene river view as possible.

"What a beautiful home," she said with awe.

"My mother has a talent for finding exceptional properties."

"She certainly does." She moved onto the veranda to admire the garden before they toured the rest. "It seems bigger than they need. Although, I guess your parents will be here for some dinners with them," she mused as she took in the dining room that sat twenty-four. "But five bedrooms?"

Each had its own bath, and there was accommodation for four in the pool house, plus a small flat for the butler over the garage. Rooms were also set aside for a nanny next to a potential nursery. All of it was decorated in clean, uncluttered lines that still managed to look warm and elegant.

"It's beautiful, but if it's super expensive—"

"It's not," he assured her, waving her into the master bedroom. Like the rest of the house, it was a soothing space with recessed lighting and had a killer view of the river.

"Dad's going to feel like a king in here."

"Um…" Time to come clean, especially since a maid ducked out of the closet, bowed and said she would finish unpacking later.

"Unpacking?" Ivy frowned and moved into the closet. Her modest belongings from Vancouver hung alongside some of the outfits she'd chosen in Singapore yesterday. Now that her designer had her size and a sense of her taste, the selection had been filled out. Parcels and bags were stacked at the back, and the price tags still hung from many of the garments.

"I thought this was a rental for my family." Exactly as he had expected, she sounded royally peeved.

"It's for you. If you approve, I'll tell Mother to finalize the paperwork."

"You're sticking me in a house here? What about all that talk about raising our baby together? What about—"

"Oh, hell. No. Ivy." He caught her flailing hand. "Until the wedding," he stressed.

"Then you'll move in here with me?" She tugged her hand free and folded her arms, looking very apprehensive.

"Okay, I thought this would be a fun surprise." He rubbed his jaw, trying not to laugh.

"It's not," she assured him stridently. "Tell me exactly what is happening. I won't spend a lifetime guessing what you're thinking and being wrong. Been there. Hated it."

He sobered and ran his tongue over his teeth. "This is too far from the city for us to live here full-time. Once we have the wedding out of the way, my mother will show you some properties in the city. That's a bigger decision, so we'll take our time. The penthouse will be perfectly comfortable until we're ready to make that leap."

That mollified her a little. "So this *is* just a rental for the wedding?"

"No." He braced himself for another pithy reaction. "I can't take you to Vancouver and collect you from your father's home, so I'm buying you one here."

"You're buying this house as a *staging* area? You really do have too much money." She shook her head.

"It's not just for the wedding. I asked Mother to find something that would make a nice retreat when we have a free weekend. A place for you to put up your overseas friends when they visit."

"Oh. Like a cottage at the lake."

"Exactly."

"I'm being sarcastic, Jun Li!" Her fists punched the air by her hips. "Any family cottage I've ever been to has had secondhand bunk beds in it, not original art and live-in staff."

"If you don't want them, fire them." He had reached the limit of his patience and walked out of the closet. "This is yours to do with however you see fit."

"Don't be ridiculous." She came flying out behind him and glared at the incomparable view. "It's not *really* mine? Because I don't know what the foreign ownership implications are. I don't have the means to pay the staff. You realize that, don't you?"

The way she flung that at him made him realize something far more important—how far apart they were in understanding one another.

"Ivy. When I said I wanted to take responsibility for you and our baby, I meant that I would ensure the safety and security of both of you. That I will use every possible tool at my disposal."

She folded her arms defensively and let her weight fall onto her back foot. "Okay. What does that mean?"

"It means this house will be yours. Outright. The funds for upkeep will be spelled out in our marriage contract along with a budget for all your staff. It will specify your living allowance, your share in the corporation and the terms of settlement should we divorce. I'm going to discuss all that with my father after I leave here. You'll have time to review and weigh in, but I suggest you hire a lawyer to review it as well."

"That's not going to endear me to your family, is it? How angry are they that I've turned up pregnant this way, forcing you to marry someone they've never even met?" She bit her lip and said in a smaller voice, "I've been terrified to ask that."

"They're so thrilled it makes me feel like a jerk that I was planning not to marry or give them a grandchild. You'll see." He moved to take her by the shoulders and dipped his chin to look her in the eye. "Now, so you won't have any other surprises, I'll also tell you I've asked my mother's assistant to set up interviews for a mirror of her own team for you. Once I'm married, we'll both be in demand as guests and hosts. You'll need an assistant, a social secretary, you already have a stylist and you'll probably want a personal shopper."

"That's not you?" she asked weakly.

He smiled. "You also need a midwife and nutritionist for the next while, and a nanny once the baby is born. Mother's decorator can help with the nurseries and any other changes you wish to make to our homes."

"That's... I mean..." Her hands came to his forearms as if she felt dizzy.

He squeezed her shoulders and tore off the rest of the bandage.

"You'll also have your own driver and bodyguards. Unfortunately, we all need them. It's the price of our success. As for the household staff, we have an inter-family agent who manages all that. If you need to make changes, your assistant will set that up. And—"

"There's more?" she squeaked. "Please stop."

"You'll have your own bank account once we're married, but use this credit card if you need anything immediately." He withdrew two from his shirt pocket, read them and replaced his own, then offered hers.

She swallowed as she looked at it. "This is

one of those 'invitation only' kind. Limitless. I saw one in Hong Kong once. How did you get one with my name on it? So fast?"

She was so cute. "It has a concierge service. I made a call, and it was waiting when we landed. There's a new phone around here, too. It should be programmed with my direct line. I'll find it and check it before I go. If you don't have any objections to this house, I'll tell Mother to go ahead with the paperwork?"

"My objections are all of the 'Are you of sound mind?' variety," she said faintly.

"Very sound. But you're looking wan. Take the afternoon to rest before I bring my parents by later. Let the staff spoil you."

"You really have to go?" She swayed slightly toward him. Her eyes were wide with uncertain invitation as she met his gaze.

It would be so easy to walk her back to the bed and lose himself in passion. So easy. Probably even healthy.

But with so much of his life fraying and peeling off in its own directions, he had to maintain a firm grip over everything, most especially himself. Just thinking about blowing off his afternoon caused the itch of angst and tension to rise in him.

He was hovering at the entrance to an unhealthy spiral and would have to make time amid the rest of his busy day to visit his doctor for a prescription. It was frustrating and lowering, especially for a man with perfectionist tendencies. It was the best thing he could do for both of them in the long run, though.

"I do have to leave." But he couldn't make himself walk away without one kiss, one *taste*...

He cupped her face so he wouldn't touch her anywhere else. And he tried to keep it to a teasing, tender kiss of parting, but her mouth flowered open beneath his. Her tongue swept across his bottom lip in explicit desire.

He instantly hardened, nearly overcome by sudden, raw sexuality. He took complete possession of her mouth, made love to her with his tongue. He wanted to strip them both naked and plunge into her like this, again and again until they exploded. Not a sensual seduction like she deserved, but animalistic mating that left them panting and sweaty and sated.

He jerked his head back, unsettled by how tenuous his grip on his control was. The less he showed, the less he would have. This had to stop here.

She was trembling, eyelids fluttering open, breath short.

When he dropped his hands and stepped back from her, she bit the lips he'd left swollen and shiny.

"What's wrong?" She sounded uncertain. Hurt.

He bit back a curse at how untenable this was and grasped for the first rationale that came to him. "I have to be able to look your father in the eye."

"My father doesn't own my sexuality." Her brows crashed together in annoyance.

"I still think it would be best to wait until the wedding." He needed time to get himself back on track.

She snorted. "My father knows how babies are made. He slept with Mom before they married."

"And how did *her* father feel about that?" he countered dryly.

"My grandfather was never told." She spoke snippily, then seemed to realize that wasn't a point that worked in her favor. She waved dismissively. "Their situation was different. My grandmother wasn't angry they slept together. She was mad they married without permission. She wanted Mom to marry someone else."

"In Canada?"

"In Hong Kong. She took Mom to visit relatives and meet him, but while Mom was out with her cousins, she met Dad. Grandma said it was just lust." Ivy pressed her mouth into a line of consternation.

That small show of disquiet in her made the floor feel soggy beneath him. Was she worrying they didn't even have that, because he wasn't throwing her onto the bed and ravishing her? He wanted to. It was taking everything in him not to reach for her, but he was also aware it would weaken the dam holding all the emotional junk he'd bottled up out of self-preservation. He was protecting her and their combined future as much as himself.

"What happened?" He had completely lost the plot, far too aware that she was withdrawing mentally and physically, hugging herself and stepping back from him.

"Grandma tried to break them up by taking Mom home. Dad followed and married her on the sly. Grandma said he only married her to immigrate." She moved to the window. "But they loved each other," she said with quiet conviction.

And that was what Ivy wanted for *her* marriage. That's why she had been quiet and blue and solemn all day. She was seeking reassurance in passion and turning away when he didn't offer it.

A slab of concrete settled over his chest as he realized he had cheated her of something he didn't know he could ever provide. He cared about the people close to him and expected he would come to cherish her the way he did the rest of his family, but she wanted the grand, romantic love that pursued someone across continents and defied parents and couldn't be resisted because it had to be.

He pushed his hands into his pants pockets. Swallowed an acrid taste of failure.

"Your father must be sympathizing with his mother-in-law at this moment, worried about *my* motives. I need to do this right, Ivy." It was the least he could do.

"Sure. Fine. Do what you have to, and I'll wait here like a good girl. Ignore that," she commanded, immediately throwing up a hand. "I'm freaking out. Staff, Jun Li? A *house*? I appreciate everything you're doing, but how am I supposed to react to any of this? I was excited when I heard my new job came with a *title*."

He relaxed a little. "You'll get used to it."

As he hovered one more second, he realized he wanted to draw her into an embrace and kiss her to reassure them both. It bothered him to leave her with this discord between them.

"Do you want me to tell the butler you're lying down?" He took a step toward the door.

"Thank you." She nodded, mouth pouted in a way that made walking away hurt like hell.

"Jun Li."

His heart tripped as he turned back. His breath caught as he took in one of the loveliest women he'd ever seen in his life. Her hair was loose around her face, and her chin came to that adorably obstinate point. Her dress hugged her shoulders and cut low across the swells of her breasts then billowed loosely to flutter around her pretty knees. The dress's mossy-green color made her skin look like honey illuminated by sunshine.

"You know what I'm getting you as a wedding gift, don't you?"

"A baby?"

"A smoothie bullet."

It took him a moment, then he recalled that was what she'd got Kevin while he'd given his old friend a house. For some reason, that very lame joke had him grinning all day.

"Your blood pressure is up a little," the midwife said the morning of the wedding. "Not much and this is a big day. I'm not worried, but we'll keep an eye on it." She made a note.

The days had flown by in a flurry of meetings and interviews, fittings and meals with friends and relatives from both sides, all visiting from around the globe. Everyone was very happy for them, and several cooed quiet asides to Ivy about how lucky she was.

She was. She might have no time alone with her husband-to-be, but that didn't mean he wasn't ironing wrinkles from her days before she even saw them. They texted frequently, and at one point he sent her a link for a nine-hundred-watt stainless steel blender.

Says it's also good for baby food?

She had bought it with her own credit card, despite its extravagant price tag, and had it sent to his penthouse with a note.

Make some congee. Let me know.

I'll use it every day, he promised in a text. Such flirts they were.

But despite learning the names of his cousins and hearing stories of his childhood, she still felt as though she was marrying blindly. Any reservations she dared whisper had been refuted by whomever she voiced them to. He was Tsai Jun Li. He was rich, gorgeous, doting and had fired one of his executives when it was revealed the man had made some derogatory remarks about Ivy carrying Jun Li's baby before the wedding had happened.

Did she not realize she was the envy of every single woman in the *world*?

She had so much more with Jun Li than she'd had with Bryant. Did it matter that they weren't in love? It would come in time. Wouldn't it?

She had run out of time to change her mind if she believed it wouldn't. She was dressed in a demure red cheongsam for the ceremony. She was so nervous, she thought she would shake the petals right off her bouquet of wine-red roses before Jun Li arrived to collect her.

There was a stir below, and she came to the top of the stairs as he entered the foyer. He wore an embroidered red Tang jacket over black trousers. He was so wickedly handsome, her knees threatened to give out.

His penetrating gaze swept up and found her. He stilled as though she was something that stole his breath. She thought his throat might have flexed with a swallow.

Some of her relatives had threatened to perform playful traditions, saying they would make him earn their surrender of her, but Jun Li only had to hold out his hand. Everyone went silent as Ivy came down the stairs as though in a spell. He linked their fingers and held their clasped hands to his chest.

"Are you ready?" he asked.

"Yes," she said breathlessly.

The trip to the government office was solemn. Their parents stood by as they spoke their vows. Ivy could hardly get hers out, she was so overcome by the power of their promises to one another.

Jun Li squeezed her hand as he spoke, as if he were trying to press each word into her skin and blood and bones. When his mouth touched hers in a brief kiss, her qualms faded away. Surely something that felt this right *was* right?

From there, they went to the home of Jun Li's parents, a beautiful beaux arts villa in the Bund. They performed a tea ceremony to serve their parents. Jun Li's mother, Mo Chou, gave Ivy a stunning gold necklace made of links shaped like ivy leaves. Some were solid, some hollow, giving it an airy, delicate look. It had a matching bracelet and earrings and was so pretty, Ivy said sincerely, "I'll treasure this always."

She was already wearing a gold hair ornament that had been worn by her mother and grandmother for their own weddings. Her father had brought it along with some rare coins and jade carvings that he had collected over the years for exactly this occasion, so he could gift them to her new husband's parents.

After a light meal, they went to the hotel, where she and Jun Li were shown into a lavish top-floor suite. Ivy's stylist had taken over one bedroom, where she had organized all Ivy's outfits for the banquet.

She helped Ivy into an elaborate qipao with a long silk train. It was embroidered down one side with gold threads and colorful flowers. Jun Li was waiting for her when she emerged. He had changed into a different red wedding tunic with embroidery similar to hers.

Moments later, when they entered the ballroom, the wave of excitement off the five hundred guests nearly felled her.

They visited every table while the guests ate, each requiring introductions and toasts. It took hours, and they disappeared several times to change. Each time, Ivy discovered Jun Li had gifted her more jewelry and he switched to a jacket that matched her own gown.

When she put on a traditional Western wedding dress and wore a necklace of diamonds, he changed into a white tuxedo. Her dark pink gown was a foil for rubies of an intense magenta color while he wore a burgundy-colored vest over a black shirt. She switched to a mermaid-style gown in buttercup yellow, sunny sapphires falling like petals over her collarbone while he appeared in a mandarin-collared jacket of muted saffron.

Finally, after the speeches were finished, Ivy put on a sleeveless cocktail dress in midnight-blue velvet. A necklace and earrings appeared that matched her engagement ring of blue and white diamonds.

"You look incredible. Edible," Jun Li told her. He dipped his head to press a kiss to the point of her bare shoulder.

Each time they'd entered the elevator, he'd complimented her. Each time, she had thanked him profusely for the jewelry.

This time she could only smile weakly. Her feet ached and her cheeks were sore from forcing herself to smile. Her voice hurt from talking, and she still had to get through sending everyone off with their wedding favors.

"Are you okay?" he asked, giving her elbow a squeeze.

"Just tired. But I can stay in bed all day tomorrow if I want to."

"That was my plan."

A blush hit her cheeks, and she looked down to hide it.

She was nervous about making love again but glad to hear some enthusiasm from him. Despite the passion that had overwhelmed her in Singapore, he'd been adamant about keeping their affection to a few tame kisses. They'd constantly been surrounded by friends and relatives, barely able to exchange private words, let alone more, but it bothered her that he hadn't even tried. The desire seemed to be all on her side, not so much on his.

"Ladies and gentlemen, our groom has arranged a special treat for you," a voice announced as they reappeared.

The ceiling opened to reveal the night sky. While everyone murmured with surprise, the first testing streak of fireworks appeared like a shooting star. Music began to play, and the colorful explosions were perfectly synchronized to the booms in the music. Everyone cheered with enjoyment.

Ivy stood in Jun Li's arms, head tilted up to watch. It was beautiful, but the roof seemed to be closing in before the show was over. Jun Li's arm tightened around her, making her feel as though he was cutting off her air because none was entering her lungs.

"Ivy!" His voice was a million miles away.

CHAPTER EIGHT

IVY WILTED IN his arms, head lolling, scaring the hell out of him.

As she crumpled, Jun Li caught her behind the legs and cradled her to his chest while he scanned for one of the physicians in attendance. As people began lowering their attention from the sky and releasing murmurs of alarm, his uncle on his mother's side—a general practitioner—hurried toward him.

"She saw her midwife this morning. She said the checkup was fine," Jun Li told him.

His uncle motioned to the dais. A screen had been set up behind the podium to provide a backdrop for the speakers. It afforded them a little privacy as Jun Li lowered Ivy onto the carpeted floor behind it.

Her eyes were already fluttering open in disoriented alarm. "What—?"

"Let him take your pulse," he told her as she instinctively tried to pull away from his uncle's hold on her wrist.

His uncle asked whether there was bleeding or cramping, questions that put a knot of sick terror in the pit of Jun Li's gut even after she dismissed them.

"No, I'm fine. I haven't eaten since this afternoon," she admitted with chagrin.

"We had food in the room." Jun Li had been snacking each time they changed and had presumed Ivy was doing the same.

"I didn't want to risk staining any of the gowns."

"They're just clothes," he muttered, but while he'd been shrugging on a new jacket, she'd been sitting to have her hair restyled and her makeup retouched.

"The midwife told me to stay hydrated, but we had so many people to meet," she continued with apology. "I didn't want to excuse myself every five minutes. Honestly, I'm fine. All the running around this week has caught up to me, that's all. Now I'm making a scene and I feel like a fool. Please let me up."

His uncle helped her sit but watched her closely. "Dizzy?"

"Mortally embarrassed."

A waiter was hovering with a phone. He asked Jun Li if an ambulance was needed.

Jun Li sent him for a rehydration drink. "Something with protein," he added, then crouched beside Ivy. "You should have told me you weren't feeling well."

"I've gone without eating and drinking before when I've been traveling or had work deadlines. I've never fainted."

"Your baby is using all of your resources now," his uncle scolded. "You have to take better care of yourself."

"I will," Ivy promised.

"*I* will," Jun Li swore.

"Can we please go back out there? Before everyone thinks this is more serious than it is? Oh, Dad, I'm fine," she said, looking past Jun Li.

He stepped out of the way so she could re-assure her father.

The music was finishing up with a finale of explosions, but the cheering had stopped. The air of concern was palpable. Jun Li moved to the podium and waited for the last notes of the music to fade before he spoke.

"Ivy is feeling the strain of the day," he told the crowd. "We are honored and grateful that you took this time to be with us today, but we'll be leaving shortly—"

The crowd gave an audible sigh of relief and beamed, clapping as Ivy came out from behind the screen to join him.

"I'm fine," she insisted and showed him the milky drink she was sipping. "I'd like to stay and see everyone off."

Her color was better, but Jun Li had a chair brought for her to sit in while their families gathered around them and guests filed by to say their good nights. No one lingered, and Ivy's soon-to-be stepsisters did most of the work in handing out the gift bags. They were shaped like sedan chairs and held handmade candies, oranges, red chopsticks engraved with his and Ivy's names, gold pendants with the double happiness symbol, and other keepsakes.

"I thought you might want one of these," Kevin said at Jun Li's elbow.

Jun Li dragged his watchful eye off Ivy to see Kevin was offering a glass of scotch.

"Thank you." Despite the many toasts in their honor today, Jun Li hadn't imbibed. He typically avoided alcohol since it was a depressant, but he accepted the drink, appreciating the stimulating bite as he sipped. "And thank you for interrupting your honeymoon to be with us today."

"We wouldn't have missed it. You two should join us in Bora Bora for a few days. Ivy could use the R and R. You too?"

Kevin was the only other person Jun Li had ever told about his long ago pregnancy debacle. He understood the pressures Jun Li had put upon himself from an early age and the load he carried today. He knew how Jun

Li's drive to succeed had a downside. Any sort of failure hit him like a northbound bus.

Kevin's new wife, Carla, was chatting with Ivy. The crowd had thinned, and everyone else was occupied in pockets of conversation. Jun Li stepped away from the line to speak more privately with Kevin.

"I saw she was looking tired, but she said she was fine. I should have listened to my gut." Jun Li was furious with himself.

"That tracks. For Ivy, I mean," Kevin said with a dry chuckle, holding up a hand. "Your instincts remain infamously sharp, and I'm surprised you ignored them. But when I worked with her in Hong Kong, I saw very quickly that she was the kind of person other people feed a sob story to so she would do their work for them. She reminds me of my sister. Doesn't know how to set limits and say no."

Like when a man asked her to come to his hotel room? Or pressured her into marriage? Jun Li's heart fishtailed in his chest.

"You'll be good for her. You're notoriously

self-sufficient. Nothing like that vampire of needs who had her throwing away a promotion in Hong Kong so he could throw *her* away. What an idiot," Kevin scoffed. "His loss was supposed to be my gain. That's why I introduced you two at our engagement party. I wanted to find a place for Ivy in my office. Thanks, by the way, for stealing her away and killing that masterful plan."

Jun Li had a flash of where he would be right now if Kevin had made that clear to him. Ivy would have been off-limits and none of this would have happened. He took a deep sip of his scotch to burn away the uncomfortable dryness that arrived in the back of his throat.

"When I saw her again a few weeks ago, I was planning to feel her out on working for me, but she asked whether you'd be coming to our wedding. She was wearing the guiltiest, most painfully casual look I've ever pretended to believe. Have you been seeing her this whole time?"

Jun Li licked his lips. "Not exactly."

"Hmm." The noise was neither pleased nor dismayed.

That shouldn't bother him, but Kevin was his closest friend. "Look, you know why I've avoided serious relationships. I felt stretched too thin as it was."

His instincts had been correct there, too. He had feared the responsibility of a wife and child would put him into a depression, and the sense of not being enough had been closing in on him for days.

"I know." Kevin gave the back of his shoulder an affectionate slap. "Ivy might remind me of my sister, but you are like a brother to me." They had never spoken frankly about why Jun Li had opened his home to Kevin even though he had felt alone for so long by then, he had come to believe he preferred it. "I want you to be happy, Jun Li. I believe Ivy could make you happy. If you let her."

His response ought to have been, *I am happy*. It was his wedding day. But he didn't know what happiness *was*. It was hard for

Jun Li to say he was even content. He experienced brief moments of satisfaction over accomplishments, which was what he'd been feeling until Ivy had fainted.

He was filled with self-criticism at not having predicted her faint. He'd been distracted, ruminating over her reaction when he had mentioned staying in bed all day. The thought of making love to her was the only thing keeping him sane through this demanding week. Once they were married, she would be *his*. He couldn't wait to make it so.

She'd looked conflicted, though.

He wasn't about to force himself on her, especially when she was passing out from low blood sugar and exhaustion.

Ivy looked over then. Her smile faltered as she met whatever severity his thoughts were putting into his expression. After a disconcerted blink, she offered a warm smile to Kevin. Kevin nodded at Jun Li and went across to wish her well.

Someone else came up to him, and Jun Li

threw himself back into thanking their departing guests while privately continuing to brood.

Ivy was still feeling sheepish over her faint when she and Jun Li entered his penthouse a short distance from the hotel. Bridal shyness accosted her. After a week when they'd begun to feel more like business partners than romantic ones, she was ready to explore a deeper, more intimate connection, but she was ridiculously self-conscious about making love again.

Everything had changed since their first time. *She* had. Their relationship had. In Vancouver she'd felt more like his equal, muscle car and five-star hotel room notwithstanding. She had known that she wouldn't see him again, so the emotional stakes had been minimized.

Now their lives were irrevocably tied. Whatever happened between them tonight would carry over into the next day and the next for the rest of their lives.

What if it wasn't like it had been in Vancouver? What if the passion was only on her side and she went off like a firecracker the way she had in Singapore, making a fool of herself?

Jun Li had been watching her like a hawk since her faint, and not in a good way. She felt as though a wall had come down between them, and she wasn't sure what to do about it.

Aside from his butler, the place was deserted. As soon as the man pointed out the refreshments he'd left for them, Jun Li dismissed him.

Ivy sank onto the sofa, trying to read her husband as he filled a bowl with soup and brought it to her.

"Are you angry with me?" she asked as she accepted the soup.

"I'm angry with myself. I could see you were tired." He sat next to her and pointed at her foot then patted his thigh.

She carefully shifted her position and set her shod feet in his lap then sipped the fragrant ginger-scented broth while he unbuckled her shoes and eased them away. He dropped them, then rubbed through the blue silk of her hose where the straps had left small indents across the tops of her feet.

"Why are you wearing shoes that are too small?"

"My feet are swollen from being on them all day."

He sighed. "I expect you to tell me when I'm asking too much of you." His grip shifted, gently crushing her arch so the tension released.

It made for a confusing contrast of dull pain and sharp relief. Of feeling like she was being punished but doted on at the same time. She bit back a groan.

"I kept thinking it was only a little bit longer—" she started to say.

"Isn't that what you thought with that other man?" He gently bent her toes back and forth. "That you only had to put up with his disregard a little longer?"

"That was different," she protested, practically shuddering as the flex and relaxation in her feet caused her whole body to melt.

"I promised I wouldn't ignore your needs. I'll be more careful with you from now on, blossom, but I need your help. I'm not a mind reader." He gave her foot another firm squeeze.

She couldn't help her moan of pleasure-pain. Her eyelids fluttered closed.

"That feels so good," she sighed.

"Finish your soup." He kept rubbing her feet while she sipped. He rolled her ankles and massaged up her calves. By the time she had drained her bowl and she set it aside, she was a puddle of flesh.

"Do you want me to run you a bath?"

"That sounds nice." Her shoulders and upper chest had been dusted with pearlescent glitter for this dress. She was dying to wash it away and lose these false eyelashes along with the rest of her makeup.

Jun Li went down the hall. She walked shoeless to the table, where she prepared a plate of finger foods they could enjoy in the tub.

When she caught up to him, he was lighting floating candles in the water-filled bowls that stood on the three stairs leading up to the tub. Bubble bath was beginning to froth in the water, releasing a calming aroma of lavender.

"You are hungry," he said wryly as he took the plate from her and set it on a shelf within reach of the tub.

"It's for both of us." She turned her back to him so he could open her zipper.

The silence that greeted her remark had her lifting her gaze to the mirror.

His profile had become very remote as he slowly slid the zip down. The freedom to draw a deeper breath was profound, but even though it was warm in here, she shivered and defensively clasped the gown to her front.

"You're not planning to join me?" Why did that hurt *so much*?

"You're tired. There's no rush," he said, very offhand, as if he didn't care one way or another if they ever made love again. It drove a fresh spike of agony through her.

Ivy had spent the last week counting down

the minutes until they would be together again, when she could discover if they still had, at the very least, the passion that had made this baby they had married for.

Throat aching, she moved to the sink and peeled off her lashes, then began to pull the decorative pins from her hair. It caused her dress to slump to her hips.

Jun Li was turned away, closing the taps on the bath. Ivy hurried to wriggle free of her dress and toss it over the back of a wooden chair. She took up the silk robe that had been artfully draped there and started to shrug it on before Jun Li saw what she was wearing.

The room was nothing but mirrors, though. He turned his head, caught her reflection from the corner of his eye and did a swift double take, swinging around and swearing under his breath.

"What?" Her heart leaped into her throat, but she acted as casual as possible as she started to close the robe over the underwear she'd chosen for his pleasure. Heaven knows, it wasn't for her comfort.

At the last second, however, a prickle of defiance stopped her from belting the robe. She turned to the mirror and held it open, cocking her head as she regarded herself.

"I chose blue to go with the dress. It's pretty with the necklace, isn't it?" The strapless bra was more of a bustier with blue satin cups and a white lace overlay that hugged her ribs. Below it, she wore blue satin cheekies with a white lace garter belt. It held up the blue hose that looked closer to black in this low light.

"You should have seen it with the shoes." She went up on her toes, noting that he was paying *very* close attention and looked rather feral as shadows appeared in his hollow cheeks.

A pulse of triumph scattered butterflies of danger within her.

She dropped back to flat feet and said, "But there's no rush. Is there?"

It was a challenge, absolutely. Probably not a wise one.

When she would have belted the robe, he appeared behind her like some sort of avenging angel and tangled his hands with hers, so she was captured in the circle of his arms. Trapped, but not crushed. Pinned by the reflection of his fierce gaze meeting hers in the glass.

"I was trying to be considerate," he growled.

"I'll tell you if I'm not up for sex."

"Will you?"

It was a dig at her driving herself into a faint earlier.

"Yes," she said petulantly.

As if to test her, he tugged the belt free and opened the robe himself, exposing her to the mirror and taking another long look over her shoulder.

The naked desire in his face made warmth run into all her erogenous zones. She shifted restlessly and became aware of his hardness against her backside. She flashed him a wary look, and he quirked a brow.

"Will you tell me if you *are*?" he asked. "Up for sex?" His voice seemed to have dropped several octaves so it reverberated from within his chest against her back.

"This underwear is a bit of a neon sign, isn't it?" she tried to joke, but she was very aware that he was still drinking her in with the most ravenous, lustful look on his face. It was both heartening and exciting but made her wonder what she had started.

"I think I'd like to hear it," he said softly, fingertips trailing across the naked skin of her midriff before he traced his thumb beneath one breast. "To be absolutely sure."

"I want to," she whispered, distracted by the sharp ache that came into her breasts. They were already swollen and tight. His light caress made her nipples sting and chafe against the satin cups.

"You want what? To be touched?" His thumb climbed higher and higher while his other hand brushed aside her hair. "Kissed?" He opened his mouth against her nape.

Her knees went soft. "Yes. Both. Everything."

"Oh, be careful what you invite, blossom." His teeth lightly scraped against the side of her neck, making her scalp tighten while she reflexively slouched into him. Her breast fell into his palm, and he gave her nipple a light pinch through the cup.

It was enough to make a sob pang in her throat, more alarm at the threat of pain than the real thing, but her reaction was quick and instinctive.

He started to jerk his hand away, but she covered it to keep it there.

"They're really sensitive," she said. "Just be gentle."

"Are they?" His touch drew patterns on the swells above the edge of the cup while his lips nibbled at her earlobe, heavy with the dangling blue diamond she was wearing. "I won't suck your nipples, then. I'll only taste and blow on them."

He blew softly against her damp earlobe. She gasped at the sensation, half-drunk with passion from a few words of a sensual promise. She tried to turn, but he didn't let her.

"Are you hurt? Do you want to stop?" His smile flashed.

"You know I don't."

"What then?"

"Keep going. Touch me. Show me what *you* want," she dared, meeting his gaze in the mirror.

"I want all of you." He held her stare while his hand went down from her breast, down her center, down, down until he cupped her mound. "I want this." He pressed his touch over her, possessively claiming her. "I want to feel you melt and hear you scream my name."

She was shaking with want, throbbing beneath the pressure of his hand.

"Open your legs," he commanded softly. "Let me touch you."

She did. He shifted his touch so his fingertips stole down the front of her cheekies. It was blatant, both of them watching as his flattened fingers petted down her sensitive flesh. The garter belt framed his caress as he rocked his hand inside the satin. Her eyelids fluttered.

"Are you breathing, blossom? I don't want you to faint again," he teased.

She was gasping with anticipation. Aching

and needy. Biting her lip as he took his time tracing into the furrow of her folds, intensifying her sensations. A rumbling noise of satisfaction tickled her ear as his touch moved freely in the moisture gathered there.

"I've wanted you for months." His mouth swept her neck again. "Since that night. It's all I've thought about. Feeling you shaking and digging your nails into me again."

Was she? One of her hands was up around his neck, the other gripped his upper arm through his sleeve. He still wore his shirt and pants, the crispness of the fabric a further stimulation through the layer of silk against her back.

"Let me watch you come apart." His touch began to roll and dip and slide against the small knot of nerves that were already dancing waves of escalating pleasure through her. "Move with me. Show me how to make it good."

She couldn't resist his command. Her hips began to rock. She ground her bottom against his hardness while he played his touch inside the satin and lace. His cheeks grew flushed with excitement as he watched them. As she saw what her pleasure was doing to him, hers increased, making their sexual play that much more erotic.

Her excitement reached breaking point. Climax swept up and over her. She called out his name and shattered in his arms.

CHAPTER NINE

FOR THE SECOND time tonight, Jun Li picked up Ivy.

This time she wasn't a dead weight in his arms. She was weak with postorgasmic lethargy and coiled her arms around his neck, offering her mouth. He spared a moment to ravage her, holding back nothing since she met his kiss with equal abandonment. Her mouth opened unreservedly beneath his. Her tongue brushed against his while she moaned and pressed the back of his head, urging him to kiss her harder.

He was so aroused, he could have taken her to the floor, but he wasn't consummating their marriage on the hard tiles of a bathroom. He dragged his head up and strode to the bedroom, where he set her on his bed. He began yanking at his clothes.

"Don't take that off," he ordered when she flicked at a clasp against the top of her hose.

"You *do* like what I'm wearing." She smoothed her hand over one knee and arranged herself more provocatively, weight propped on an elbow. She hooked her other thumb in the top of her underpants. "These don't come off unless I release the garter straps." She crooked her knee up and popped the second clasp.

"Let me do it, then." His guttural voice didn't sound like his own. He was sinking into a barbaric one-track head space that originated nowhere near his head. It was the abandonment of control he'd been avoiding, and it took everything in him to keep himself this side of civilized.

He rolled her over, nearly dying at the way the underside of her plump cheeks was outlined in blue satin and white lace. He wanted to bite those tender, buttercream-colored swells.

"I'm going to give you a special allowance to spend exclusively on lingerie," he informed her as he blindly kicked away his trousers. "I should have written it into our contract as a marital requirement."

She propped herself on her elbows and gave him a sultry look over her shoulder, kicking one foot. "You realize how much power you're giving me? If I dent the car or burn the cookies, I'll buy a thong before I tell you."

"Dent all my cars." He was naked and so aroused, he was shaking.

He braced one knee on the bed to survey the lissome shape that had dominated his fantasy life for months. Finally, he could touch her again. He did, running his hand over the silk that hugged her calf until he arrived at the back of her thigh. He caressed all the naked skin he could find, running his fingers beneath the tension of the straps and the lace of her underwear, making her squirm and lift her plump cheek into his touch.

He wanted to cover her and have her like this. In a thousand ways. Kiss and lick and thrust and claim.

He could. He had a lifetime to explore all

the ways they could drive each other mad. It was mind-blowing.

He kissed her shoulders and discovered the lace that hugged her ribs had a dozen hooks closing it. He nuzzled her spine as he released them one by one, enjoying the way she flexed and writhed and caught her breath.

"I want to eat you alive. Every inch." He ran his mouth over her naked back as he fully exposed it, up to her nape, where she seemed particularly sensitive, and back down her spine to where it dipped into her lower back.

"Quit teasing. I'm dying," she moaned.

He laughed but saw she was still supporting herself on her arms as though to keep her weight off her breasts. He flicked open the clasps at the backs of her thighs and rolled her face up, dragging the bra from where it had fallen between them and throwing it away.

"Sore?" he asked as he grazed a knuckle along the side of one breast.

"A little. It feels good to be out of that." She gave a luxurious stretch.

Damn, she was beautiful. Most of her wore

a fading summer tan, but her naked breasts were a subtle gold with light brown nipples, pert as toffee candies. He wanted to suck each one into his mouth, savor and play and make her melt, but he remembered his promise and only anointed one with his tongue then blew softly.

Her legs pinched together as though she was trying to protect herself from the intensity of sensations. He set his thigh across them, teasing himself with the feel of the hose and a stray garter buckle digging into the inside of his leg.

Her breath hitched as he used his weight to control her. He glanced into her eyes to see if she was uncomfortable with his light dominance and saw excitement glowing there. A charge of power and sexual thrill went through him.

Oh yes. She enjoyed a little constriction, didn't she? It was absolutely his pleasure to deliver it.

He shifted atop her, pinning her wrists beside her head while holding his weight off her chest with his elbows. His legs closed on the outsides of hers and he held her trapped and still, though she tried to arch up into him.

"Careful, blossom." He nibbled his lips against hers and kissed her chin before lifting a little so he could admire her quivering breasts again. "These are mine now. I won't let them get hurt."

"Is that mine?" Her thighs twitched, stimulating his throbbing length where he had nestled it in the valley above the tops of her hose where her legs were pressed together.

"All yours." He pulsed his hips, teasing both of them with a small stab against the satin protecting her plump, tender flesh. The satin that covered her mound, radiant with the heat of her desire, caressed his swollen tip and nearly turned him inside out.

"I'm claiming the rest of what's mine first," he said with possessive intent. He licked into the small hollow at the base of her throat and kissed across her upper chest. He nuzzled and blew softly and tantalized her nipples until she was moaning beneath him, hips trying to rock and wrists turning in his grasp.

"I'm ready," she gasped. "You don't have to…"

"Oh, I do." He rose onto his splayed knees, keeping her legs trapped between his own.

She was a vision of sensuality, hair spilling around her, arms weak against the covers, breasts hitching and stomach quivering. The scorching way she looked him over, gaze arrowing downward until she fixated on his erection, nearly burned his skin from his bones. She licked her lips, and he nearly lost it on the spot.

He had wanted to take his time nudging the scrap of lace down to expose her a centimeter at a time, teasing both of them. He didn't have that kind of discipline left. He shifted off her and dragged her underwear away, taking a legging of hose with it.

She opened her legs and held up her arms invitingly, but he had to—*had to*—taste her. He slid down the bed and curled his arm around her thigh, taking soft bites of her smooth skin while she threaded her fingers into his hair and gave a ragged cry at the first press of his mouth against her hot, sweet core.

He could have lingered there forever, but she was more than ready to take him, and he was so drunk on the essence of her, he rose over her again.

No condom, he realized as the reflexive thought flitted into his mind. She was his and he was hers, nothing between them but the heat of their passion.

He pressed into her. Her soft flesh briefly resisted, then he was enveloped by paradise. Swallowed. Engulfed. Her legs closed around his waist, and her arms looped around his neck.

It took everything in him to keep a leash on himself. To be gentle. To thrust with measured power when he wanted to lose himself in wild, unfettered abandonment. He wanted to imprint himself on her for all time. That's how it had been before. The urge was even stronger now. She was his and he wanted her to know it. *His.*

If anything, his enforced restraint made the act even more intense. He was shaking with effort, his entire body one live nerve that was being stroked by her soft hands and hugged by her strong thighs. Her gasping breaths were painting his shoulder and her heat, her incredible heat, was bathing him in more pleasure than he'd ever known.

"Deeper," she gasped. "Don't stop, Jun Li. Don't stop. Keep going—" Her cries of culmination struck his ears and stripped him of his last vestige of control.

He straightened his arms and threw back his head, pressing into her one final time as he gave himself up to her.

Ivy woke a few hours later, eyes clogged with the makeup she hadn't removed. She slipped from the weight of Jun Li's arm, feeling very languid and lovely. She was still wearing the garter belt, and the dangling straps titillated her as she walked to the bathroom. She let it drop to the tiles as she entered.

The tub water had gone cold, but most of

the candles were still burning. She left the lights off, flicked the knob to release the water, then brushed her teeth. She rubbed cleansing cream all over her face before starting the shower.

As she stood with her face turned up to the stream, rinsing away cream and makeup in one go, Jun Li asked in a rumbling voice, "Need help in there?"

"Always," she invited and skimmed the water out of her eyes.

She turned to face him as he entered the huge glass cubicle. The candlelight picked up glints on his jaw and amid the shadows of hair on his chest.

"You're covered in the sparkles I was wearing." She tried to brush them away with her damp hand, but it didn't work.

"I believe that's the magic of sex within the sanctity of marriage." His hair was rumpled, his eyelids heavy with satisfaction. "Let's hope it never wears off."

She chuckled throatily as he dragged her close and kissed her.

They began to soap one another and he grew steely between them, but just when she thought things were going to turn very magical, he stilled. His hand had been on her abdomen but lifted away while he stared intently at her belly button.

"I'm starting to show, I know." Her hand had no hope of hiding it, but she covered her navel anyway.

"I was too distracted by the sexy underwear to notice earlier."

"The dress designer was going crazy trying to downplay it."

"Why?" He gave her a perplexed look.

"Well, it's not very sexy, is it?"

"I assure you this curviness suits you. You're sexier than ever." He brought his slippery hands up to gently cup her breasts. In the golden glow of the steam-filtered candlelight, his expression was very somber. "It makes me realize the baby is real, though."

She choked on a disbelieving laugh. "The paternity report didn't clue you in?"

"I gave it to my parents without reading it,"

he said with a distracted shrug. "I had all the proof I needed. Rationally." He waved at his own head, then his tongue touched his bottom lip, and his expression grew introspective.

The shadows of reservations lingering behind his eyes worried her.

"Are you…" She hesitated, fearful of the answer. "Are you happy about the baby?"

"I'm still in shock," he said with candor. "Concerned about both of you. I'm constantly thinking about everything that needs to be done before the baby arrives." He absently circled his palm in the soapy bubbles at her hip. "I have no idea what sort of father I'll make, which is the kind of uncertainty and lack of confidence I hate most. I prefer to tackle things that are only a matter of reading a few books to master. There's no way to know or prepare for what we face."

It wasn't the effusive joy she had hoped for, but it was honest and gave her some insight into his thoughts at least.

"Are you?" he asked. "Happy?"

She nodded helplessly, smile wobbling with emotion. "From the first minute, even though I was terrified and knew you would be furious."

"Confused," he corrected.

"I assumed I would have to do it on my own, which was scary, but I always wanted to be a mother. I was glad I was pregnant by you. I didn't regret anything about our night together so I couldn't regret that it resulted in a baby." She bit her lip, hesitating before she admitted, "I was glad it gave me an excuse to see you again. I wanted to."

A subtle flinch tightened his expression.

"I wanted to see you, too," he said, but she could tell it was hard for him to reveal that. "But I wasn't planning any sort of future with anyone. I didn't want to lead you on. This…" He waved at the steam around them. "Marrying for practical reasons… I'm confident I can meet your needs and give you a good life, but I'm not sure I can be everything you want. That concerns me."

"You mean…love?"

"Yes."

Her arms seemed to tremble all the way to her fingertips. In these last hours, she had begun to believe something wonderful was around the corner. Now it slipped out of sight.

She wanted to say *Why did you marry me, then?* But she could turn that question on herself, and the answer was because she was falling for him.

"You don't have to be anything but who you are." She spoke bravely, trying to convince both of them. "A marriage isn't a project with deliverables and milestones and once it's commissioned, it runs like clockwork. It's something we'll build over time."

His mouth relaxed. "Am I going to have to learn more about what you do for a living so I can liken our marriage to analyzing compliance?"

"You do not want our marriage to be anything like my work," she assured him. "I make a career of being a wet blanket. I say, 'You can't do that or you'll risk a lawsuit.' Then people tell me to leave the room because I've ruined their party. And something tells me you know that." She pinched at his belly, determined to return to a lighter mood and a sense of accord. "All the top guns I've ever known have ducked into the men's room when they've seen me coming."

"Because plausible deniability is a very useful thing to possess." His smile flashed.

"Well, you're missing out on valuable information. For instance, I happen to know you're not supposed to talk about work on your wedding night. There are other things you're legally required to do."

"Legally?" he repeated. "Educate me. I don't want to overlook a single directive."

She wanted to make a joke about being unable to deny the plausible evidence that was hard against her slippery belly, but their gazes tangled, and such giddy happiness arrived, she couldn't speak.

He cupped her damp cheek and kissed her, tender and profound at once, erasing all other thoughts in her mind except the desire to touch and taste and steep herself in the pleasure they gave one another.

She wound up taking hold of his steely length, smoothing her hands over him in the rain of the warm water, saying, "Let me show you."

She drew him with her as she backed up and sat on the bench. Then she took him in her mouth, making him hiss and brace a hand on the glass. As steam gathered around them, she stroked the iron strength of his thighs and caressed his buttocks and reveled in completely dismantling him.

Afterward, he took her back to bed and did the same to her. Twice.

They both passed out then, sleeping late, but woke to make love again. It went on like that for the whole of the following day, both of them immersing themselves in one another. It was tender and playful and sexy, and it was a long time before Ivy feared again that she might not get everything she needed from this marriage.

* * *

Jun Li had had a handful of long-term relationships. Aside from taking a date to company-sponsored charity galas, he had mostly kept his romantic life separate from work. Because of that, he expected Ivy's presence at his business dinners to distract him and divide his attention.

On the contrary—she proved to be a surprising asset at the mixers and networking events they began to attend together. She slid effortlessly between the small talk of social niceties and the meaty business discussions that were often held in multiple languages.

In fact, when they were flying back to Singapore after breaking ground on a port project, she said, "If I heard correctly that some of the project is financed with cryptocurrency, I'd double-check your financing contracts on how that's to be reported. The EU has been updating their regulations. You don't want to fall into noncompliance. The fines are huge."

He did, caught a potential oversight that would have put them grossly over budget if they'd been fined for it and replaced a less competent officer with one who had Ivy's proactive attitude and attention to detail.

When they visited Hong Kong, she introduced him to the president of the bank where she had earned a reputation for being conscientious and scrupulously honest, once recommending the termination of a trader who had arrogantly tried to avoid her audits. She had rescued the bank from the jaws of a damaging scandal, and the president still bemoaned the fact she'd transferred back to Canada rather than take the promotion he'd offered her.

"Thank you for making a point of introducing us," Jun Li said when they were back at his villa in the Peak. "He's an invaluable connection. There's a certain snobbery when it comes to old money versus new." And occasional suspicions over how new money had been made. "Now he knows I'm legitimate."

"Yes, I know. That's why I did it."

Her smile bordered on smug, but the sly way she slanted it at him caused a hard pulse inside him. Her face was rounder these days, her skin wearing the glow the pregnancy books talked about. Her breasts and backside were something men sneaked glances at, himself included. From behind, she didn't even look pregnant, just sumptuously curvy.

"Are we keeping track?" she asked as she used her hands to frame the small pot filling out her front. "This evening it was unanimous that the way I'm carrying indicates a boy."

"We could ask the doctor." He averted his gaze and shrugged out of his jacket, throwing it over the back of a nearby chair.

"Where's the fun in that?"

Where was the fun in any of it, he almost asked, but bit back what would sound very cruel. The more obvious her pregnancy became, however, the less he could deny his impending fatherhood. He didn't want to, not really. It was just that when he let himself contemplate how much more his life would change than it already had, his sense of control eroded to the point he was only grasping grains of sand. Everything else was slipping through his fingers.

It didn't matter that Ivy was fitting into his life so seamlessly. A baby would be different. No matter how much he read, he didn't feel prepared. In fact, he was beginning to think reading about it fed the dark clouds that danced around his periphery, threatening to close in on him.

"Can you please?" She turned her back on him and held up her hair.

He unclasped her necklace and opened the zip on her dress.

"I'm going to miss this," she said as he impulsively placed a kiss on the spot where her neck met her shoulder.

"What?"

"You. Traveling with you and…being husband and wife." He'd left her alone for a night or two here and there, but she'd accompanied him on his longer trips throughout Asia. She was starting her third trimester, though. Her midwife had advised this be her last flight of nonessential travel. "It's felt like a honey-moon."

"Now I feel really guilty that we've put off taking one until after the baby comes."

"That's not why I said it. I wanted you to know that I like being with you." Her smile was offset. Self-conscious. The way she searched his eyes made his chest tighten.

He was going to miss her, too. That's what he should have said. He wasn't letting himself think about how he would feel, though. He'd been leaning on old, not very healthy habits of pressing negative feelings deep into his subconscious rather than dealing with them.

"You're tired, though." He saw it in the way she stole catnaps every chance she got. "It's time you began to take it easy."

She made a noise of reluctant agreement, then tilted another look up at him. It held the sort of invitation that made his blood heat.

"I'm not *too* tired."

Good, because his appetite for her never seemed to abate. Nor hers for him, which was intensely gratifying. She tended to be on top these days since it was more comfortable for her. No matter how they made love, he was transported to a euphoria that left him spent and satiated. Even the feel of her damp skin against his in the aftermath, when her hair tickled his jaw and he was afraid to move because he didn't want to wake her, was deeply satisfying.

She nudged him in the side, then drew in a startled breath even as he realized her arm was across his waist. She hadn't nudged him. The baby had.

"Did you feel that?" she asked with a sleepy laugh and tried to bring his hand to her bump. "Our little gymnast woke me up."

"Mmm. No wonder you're so tired, building us a gold medalist." His heart was clogging his throat. He extricated himself and left the bed. "Try to go back to sleep. I'm going to get a little work done."

She made a noise of disappointment but drew a pillow into the space he'd occupied and sighed, dropping back to sleep in an instant.

While he berated himself. This was ridiculous. He should not be this unsettled by something so natural. He wanted to crawl straight back into bed beside her, but there was something grimly familiar about the looming emptiness of leaving her behind once they returned home. It made him wary of allowing himself to become too attached to her presence next to him as he slept.

He told himself it was better that he return to his mostly solitary life before he couldn't face it without feeling like a limb had been amputated, but that was exactly how it felt. From the moment he installed her in his penthouse in Shanghai and left for New York, the pit of his gut became heavy with dread. He moved through his days as though walking through gelatin.

He hadn't started his medication. That was the problem. It had some unpleasant side effects, so he had done what he had scolded Ivy for doing. He had put up with a few more days of feeling worked up and overloaded with apprehension and self-doubt, suffered a little longer and a little longer, hoping it would go away.

Once the wedding had been behind them, his symptoms had evened out into something he thought he could handle, but he was missing the hell out of her now.

He was a grown man, far beyond the age where he should be suffering terminal homesickness and missing a wife he'd only had for ten weeks.

He didn't want to feel this tearing need to be in two places. It was impossible. Painful. It wasn't as though his responsibilities away from her were unimportant. Given the proposed expansion into aeronautics, there was only so much he could delegate. Much of the decision making rested on him.

This sense of dependence on her was an additional stressor. This was why he hadn't wanted a wife and child. They were people he had to worry about, but also people he had to worry about being *without*.

Wrapped around all this was the knowledge that he wouldn't feel this resentment and irritation, wouldn't be brooding this hard when he ought to be paying attention in a meeting, if he had started taking his damned pills when they were prescribed to him.

"Sir." His assistant tapped his shoulder and showed him his phone with an incoming call from Ivy. He had tried her earlier, before this presentation, but her assistant had said she was lying down.

"I have to take this," he said, rising and swiping to accept the call as he left the boardroom.

"I'm sorry I missed you earlier," she said, sounding tired. "I feel silly for calling, but I promised I would tell you if I wasn't feeling well. I don't."

"What's wrong? Have you called the midwife?"

"She's here now. She said my blood pressure is up a bit, which is weird because I was reading a book, not doing anything strenuous. She's not *worried* worried, but she wants me to go to the clinic for a few tests as a precaution. I have a headache, too. I think I picked up a bug. I don't mean to worry you. I just wanted you to know."

"Do you want me to come home?"

"No. I'm sure it's fine. I just wanted you to know."

"Ivy." Everything in him had gone very still. "What do you need from me right now? Be honest."

There was such a long pause, he almost spoke her name again to be sure the call hadn't dropped. Then he heard her ask, very quietly, "Will you please come home?"

His heart flipped over in his chest, and his mouth went dry.

"I will," he said unsteadily, instantly repeating to himself the lies she had served him. He was sure it was fine. "I'll text once I'm in the air. You text as soon as you have news."

"I feel like I'm making a fuss over nothing. You really don't mind?"

"I really don't." In one way, he was glad for the excuse to go to her, but it was the worst possible reason. Asking for him was killing her, he could tell. She would only do it if, deep down, she truly felt something was wrong. "I'll see you soon."

"Okay. Thank you." She sounded subdued, not like herself at all.

He ended the call and reentered the board room long enough to excuse himself from the rest of the week's meetings and presentations. He could see the faces twisting with annoyance over the delay, but he turned his back on it, discovering he cared very little what they thought of his departure.

Two hours later he was in his private jet, reaching cruising altitude. He texted Ivy to let her know.

She texted back.

They think it's preeclampsia.

He looked up the term, read for fifteen minutes, then went to his stateroom and cracked the childproof cap on his prescription.

CHAPTER TEN

BED REST.

It could be worse—that was what Ivy kept telling herself. It was a mild case of pre-eclampsia, so she wasn't hospitalized, but she was only allowed to move from her bed to the sofa or a lounger on the terrace. She had to lie on her side and drink a million glasses of water and give samples to the midwife so often, she felt like a pincushion. She was scheduled for an ultrasound every week and had to wear a fetal heart rate monitor at different times to reassure everyone that things were not escalating.

Two weeks in, so far so good, but Ivy had to work at not stressing out over what "escalating" would mean: early delivery. They were already talking about inducing labor at thirty-four weeks. She had crossed into thirty today.

Every minute was a slightly better chance for their baby, so she was doing everything she could to buy them that time.

Which meant four more weeks of watching mindless sitcoms and reading all the romance novels she had saved to her e-reader over the last several years. She'd been trying to find time to conquer her digital to-be-read pile, but it was hard to concentrate. Every day her father offered to leap on a plane, but for what purpose? So he could pace the house restlessly the way her husband was doing? Setting her nerves on edge?

It wouldn't be so bad if she could occupy herself with continuing to shop for nursery items, but she didn't want to tempt fate.

Maybe Jun Li felt the same. She wouldn't know because he didn't want to talk about the baby. Or even *to* the baby. Yesterday, he had caught her singing to her bump. She had asked him if he wanted to join in or tell the baby what a silly mom it had.

He had stiffened and dismissed the suggestion very quickly, saying he had a call to return. When she had asked him about work later, he said, "What call? Oh. It was fine."

There hadn't been a call. She was sure of it. Why would he lie? In so many ways, he was the height of attentiveness, but there was this *wall* between them, one that had arrived with her diagnosis. When she had been traveling with him, she'd thought they were falling in love. Now, she wondered if he felt anything toward her at all.

Brooding, she told him she was going to nap.

He came up a little while later to check on her, found her awake and reading, so he fetched his laptop.

"Just go to work," she blurted, unable to deal with his mixed signals any longer.

"I am working," he claimed, but he set aside the laptop and rose from the chair to look out the window.

He wasn't working effectively or efficiently or even literally now that she'd spoken to him. She could tell he was agitated. He wasn't sleeping any better than she was, and she saw him chew an antacid several times a day.

"I'm glad you aren't traveling, but you could at least go in to your office. It's only a couple of hours back if you need to come home. I'll move to the penthouse if you want."

"The midwife and clinic are closer to this house. You need to be here, and I'm managing well enough working remotely. Quit trying to solve a problem that doesn't exist."

"I *am* a problem that exists, and I feel guilty about it," she muttered, plumping the pillow beneath her cheek.

"Why? Did you do something to make this happen?"

"No." She hated when he logicked her out of a perfectly good sulk. "But there's nothing that either of us can do. Your hovering doesn't change anything, so you should go to work."

"Ivy." He came to stand over her, hands hooked on his hips. "I am a grown man who makes his own decisions about whether to go to work or hover over his wife. If you want me to work in the other room, say so and I will."

"I want you to tell me you're angry. Or that you begrudge that I got pregnant. Tell me you regret sleeping with me."

He tucked his chin. "Is that how *you* feel?"

"No." Her heart thunked as she realized she had started a far more sobering conversation than she had meant to. She couldn't look at him, but she had to know. "I keep thinking you must resent me, though. I'm just this lump that lies around making demands."

"I feel none of those things. I'm concerned for both of you and angry with my inability to help, but I regret nothing." He sank onto the edge of the bed. "I know that relying on me is hard for you, but I hope you know me well enough by now to believe I would hire someone to fetch your socks if I didn't want to do it for you."

She couldn't help a small "pfft" of laughter, because it was such an arrogantly truthful statement. She did know that much about him, but not a lot more. That was what was bothering her. She didn't know what he was thinking or feeling.

"What is this really about, hmm?" He rubbed her arm. "I can see you're miserable and frightened. I can't fix that. I can't even tell you not to feel those things. They're warranted. All I can do is be here so you know you're not alone."

Why did he have to be so freaking *perfect*? If she had had doubts about whether she was falling for her husband, they incinerated as her heart practically exploded with love for him. It was so powerful, her eyes stung with the force of the emotion. She had to bite her lips together to keep them from quivering.

"You play your cards so close to your chest." She caught his hand, needing to touch her lips to his knuckles, needing to give this thing happening inside her a small outlet. "I'm never sure how you feel." *How do you feel about* me?

She was too frightened of the answer to ask it aloud. It had been a lot easier to feel confident about how he regarded her when she had felt more like a partner in this marriage. When her own feelings had merely been developing, not filling her to brimming. When she'd been able to *show* him—

"Do you want sex?" she asked with dawning realization.

"What?" He pulled his hand away. "Where did that come from?"

"You're so edgy. Is it because we can't make love? We could get creative. Figure something out." She wanted—needed—to feel close to him.

"You're determined to have a fight today, aren't you?" He spoke with indignant wonder. "I'm offended that you think I would ask my sick wife, who is barely moving so she can keep our child alive, to perform sexual favors. There is a perfectly good shower in there if I feel a need for an orgasm."

"So I'm just a plumbing device?"

"Now you're being horrible. We're not talking about this." He rose.

"I need to know how you feel, Jun Li!" Frustrated tears arrived to wet her lashes.

"You think I can't sense you pulling away? You're doing it right now. We were so happy when I was traveling with you. Weren't we?" Maybe she was deluding herself.

"This is a stressful and difficult time. Of course neither of us is happy."

Another nonanswer that quashed her confidence in his feelings toward her.

"I was afraid to marry you because I thought the baby was all we had between us," she reminded him. "But if that's true, what happens if...if..."

"No." He used the sternest tone she'd ever heard from him.

Fractures were working their way across her heart, though, spreading outward, making her entire being ache with anguish. She sniffed back the tears pooling in her sinuses.

"Stop. Ivy, no. Shh. Stop thinking that." He slid onto the bed and gathered her in gentle arms. Held her. Enveloped her. "Don't go there, blossom." His voice softened as he crushed her to his chest. "Stay here. Stay right here with me. We're all okay right now. Hmm?"

His hands stroked over her from crown to tailbone, grounding her and reassuring her as she fought back the wraiths and demons that were trying to steal her faith that her long-held dream of a family would come true.

"I'm really scared," she admitted, cold to the marrow of her bones.

"I know." His arms tightened. "I can't allow myself to fear, though. I can't let you see any doubt in me. If I'm turning away, it's because I don't want you to see anything but strength in me. And belief in our best outcome."

"Oh, Jun Li." Oddly, she felt a compulsion to reassure *him*. She curled herself closer, so the bump of their baby was nestled securely between them.

His touch faltered briefly before he continued petting her hair.

She tilted her head back to see up into his face. "You're doing it again." Dejected, she shifted back an inch so her bump wasn't touching him.

He made a noise of reluctance before he admitted, "I feel guilty. I don't regret sleeping with you. Never. But I feel responsible for what you're going through."

"You shouldn't. It's no one's fault." She had already run through the gamut with the doctor. This was one of those complications that could strike any pregnancy.

He rolled away for a tissue and handed it to her. As she used it to mop beneath her eyes, he sat up with his back to her. Doing it *again*.

She sighed.

"I know," he said, voice not quite even. He kept his back to her, rubbing his hands restlessly on his thighs. "There's something I've been keeping from you. I want to tell you, but it's difficult to talk about."

Her heart clunked. A chill froze her motionless. "What?" Her heart began to pound so hard she worried it was bad for the baby.

"I'm taking an antidepressant."

It was so far from anything she had expected—her mind had gone straight to divorce, cheating, terminal illness—she didn't know what to say.

"I had no idea," she stammered. "I mean, you've never left a bottle around or anything."

"I only started taking them again since..." He glanced over his shoulder and nodded at how she was lying on the bed. "I didn't like hiding it, but I didn't want you to think getting married and becoming a father has made me depressed."

"Has it?"

She watched his profile wince. "Kind of."

She stifled her gasp of hurt but felt the tendons in her neck flex.

"This is why I didn't want to tell you." He shifted so he was angled to face her. "I'm not sure I'm capable of the kind of happiness you want me to feel, Ivy. I'm wired to worry about what will cause *un*happiness. Once I start down that road, it's all I see. Heaviness and darkness. When I'm in control of my life, those shadows fade."

"But I showed up and you couldn't control this."

"Exactly. I got through our wedding without medication and thought I would be able to handle starting our life together without falling back on it."

Got through? She had to swallow another knot of agony forming in her throat. A sensible part of her understood this wasn't about her, but it still hurt to think of herself as something he *endured*.

"But when this complication happened…" For one brief second, torment flashed across his expression. His anguish was so tangible, it made her feel small for thinking he wasn't as deeply invested in this pregnancy as she was.

He smoothed his expression, and his mouth quirked. "If I'm on the pills, I worry the appropriate amount. The darkness is there, but at the edges. It doesn't take over. Maybe I'm still worrying a little more than necessary, which is why I'm hovering." He rubbed the backs of his knuckles on her upper arm. "But if I wasn't taking the pills, I would risk a far more serious depression and be no use to you at all."

His hand went back to his thigh as he regarded her. The wall was up again, but she saw it for the defense mechanism it was.

She reached to cover his hand. "And you knew what was happening because…"

"I've been here before." He nodded.

"In Vancouver." All the pieces were coming together.

"Yes. That's why Kevin came to live with me." He caught her fingers in a warm grip, but his mouth flattened.

"It's okay. I'm not judging you. Tell me as much or as little as you want."

After a moment, he pressed her hand under his, sandwiching it against his hard thigh.

"I'd been living alone for years and didn't really have any friends. I didn't understand that depression made the idea of making friends feel like too much work, like no one would want to be my friend. I came out of class one day and there was a flyer on my windshield about mental health. It said, 'Are you suffering from?' and had a list. I ticked every box." He snorted, but there was no humor in it.

"There were numbers for counseling and meeting times for group therapy. I was standing there thinking I should do something, but already knew I probably wouldn't. Classic symptom," he said in a rueful aside. "Then Kevin came up to me. His car was parked next to mine, and I was so embarrassed to be caught with that thing in my hand."

"You shouldn't be." She squeezed his thigh and slithered closer.

"I know. But he must have seen how guilty I looked. He said he answered phones at the counseling office if I ever wanted to talk. He called me 'one of the quiet ones,' the ones he worried about. I didn't even realize he was in two of my classes, I was that checked out of the world around me. But while I was standing there feeling like a tool, I noticed he had pillows and blankets in his back seat. He said he stayed late to help at the group sessions, then had morning classes, so he slept in his car half the week. I had never invited anyone into my house, but I said I had a room he could sleep in if he wanted to. He followed me home and stuck around for two years."

"And helped you?"

"He did. Not because he'd taken training sessions on mental health support, but because he was a friend. He went with me to the doctor and asked about my life and dragged me to the beach and cooked so I ate properly. None of it was a silver bullet, but it added up over time until I was much healthier."

She wanted to ask if the pregnancy scare in high school had started it. That might explain why he seemed to be holding back on bonding with the baby. And her.

I'm not sure I'm capable of the kind of happiness you want me to feel.

"You never told your parents about any of it?"

"You do know me." He cradled her jaw and ran his thumb across her cheek. "You have the softest skin," he noted absently. "I want my lips against some part of your body every minute of every day. I want to kiss you and make love to you and, yes, I am definitely missing that, blossom. But…" He sighed and moved his hand to her hip, shifting his gaze to the headboard. "These pills have side effects. Insomnia, heartburn, muscle tension, dry eyes. Erectile dysfunction. That's another reason I put off starting them," he said wryly.

"Oh. So you can't…?"

"I can. But it's not as… Let's talk about that when it's relevant," he dismissed. "Most of the side effects will settle down after a while, and hopefully our lives will, too. Then I can wean off the pills and my little issues won't matter."

They weren't little, but at least they weren't as dire as she'd feared.

"Thank you for telling me all this." She squeezed his thigh again. "It helps to know what's going on for you. I'm sorry I pressured you to talk about something so private."

"You're my wife. Keeping it from you bothered me. I don't want secrets between us." He leaned down to kiss her.

It was sweet and soft and tender and made all her love glow like a dawn sun inside her.

When they broke apart, she had to say it. *Had to.* It had been building for so long, and now he'd opened himself up, letting her see his most vulnerable inner self.

"I love you."

A light flared in his eyes before his expression shuttered, hiding it. Denying it?

She quickly closed her eyes, ignoring the way his rebuff sheared off a layer of her heart. "It's okay if you don't want to say it back, but I couldn't keep it in any longer."

"Ivy." He spoke in a shaken voice and set his hand on the side of her neck, where her pulse probably throbbed against the heel of his palm hard enough to alarm him.

"Honestly." She brought his palm to her mouth. "It's okay. I just needed you to know. No secrets." Her smile was unsteady as she peeked at him.

He didn't smile back. His brow was tortured. "Blossom, I don't know if I'm capable of that sort of love." His tone was laden with those painful words—*no secrets.*

Her heart gave a wounded cry, but she understood him better now. "I know."

She was trying to ease his tension by letting him know she didn't blame him, but he flinched and the lines of agitation in his face deepened.

The anguished silence between them might have dragged out for hours, but the butler texted to say the midwife had arrived.

"The other woman in my life," Ivy said with a weak smile. She was actually grateful to have her. The woman had become a close friend. She was the kindest, most thorough and confidence-inspiring person in the world.

Jun Li smiled faintly and went downstairs to bring her up to Ivy.

CHAPTER ELEVEN

"It MAKES ME wonder if this baby is all we have."

All the pills in the world couldn't drown out Ivy's vulnerable words.

Jun Li heard them on repeat in his head, along with, *"I love you. I couldn't keep it in any longer."*

She had humbled him with that. With the fact she had felt so deeply about him for a while and kept it to herself. She humbled him every day as she took every smidge of the doctor's and midwife's advice to heart, accepted treatment from his mother's acupuncturist and choked down Chinese medicine once the specialist okayed her to supplement with it.

She was quietly fighting with everything in her to give their baby its best chance.

Because she feared the baby was all they had between them.

That wasn't true at all, but his damned dark brain kept dredging up those same fears he hadn't let her voice. If they didn't have the baby, he would be devastated. More than he could articulate. So would she, and there was no way he could protect her from that sort of pain. The threat of it was turning him inward to brood.

And he was bottling everything so he wouldn't spill any on Ivy and scare the hell out of her. His medication could only do so much. He would need the sort of tranquilizer that dropped a bull elephant to really do the job.

Somehow her acceptance of his limitations where love was concerned kept stabbing through all his best efforts to numb his emotions, though. He couldn't help wondering if he was fighting on two different fronts. Maybe he was still trying to protect himself after that youthful offering of his heart had turned so painful.

For years, he had lumped all that dark time in Canada together as one bleak episode that he had firmly put behind him. Where was the use in picking apart those years to find which scars belonged to which injuries? That could crack the urn where he was keeping all his suppressed emotions.

He was compelled to do something tangible for Ivy, though. Something that demonstrated he did care for her, more than he knew how to express.

That's what had brought him to his parents' home in the Bund today.

"Jun Li," his father greeted him with mild surprise as he joined Jun Li in the office that was dusted daily but otherwise no longer saw much use. "Ivy?" he asked with concern.

"As well as we can expect. Her blood pressure has been coming up in the last week. They gave her medication the other day to help the baby's lungs develop. We're hoping she lasts to thirty-six weeks, but it's likely they'll have to induce labor soon."

His father made a noise of concern, but they

were interrupted briefly as tea was brought in. His father invited him to sit, and they settled into the comfortable chairs, poured tea and took a few moments to appreciate it.

"You want to discuss a restructure with the company?" his father prompted.

"I do." A cleaving sensation pried in his chest. Jun Li felt disloyal and ungrateful even bringing this up, but when he looked into the future, he saw Ivy and their baby first, not the company. "I'd like to cancel the expansion. And sell off all but the core infrastructure division."

His father's brows went up. After a moment, he brought his tea to his lips and sipped.

"Something will fail otherwise. *I* will." Jun Li abandoned his cup and rose to pace. "It galls me to say I can't do it all. I know you built and managed all this while supporting a wife and child, but I can already tell that something will suffer if I don't narrow my focus. Ivy and the baby will suffer. I've been forced to delegate more while Ivy has been so ill, but that's not sustainable. The expansion would be a feather in our cap, but I find myself asking, How much is enough? How does it provide more security than we currently have? Isn't it more prudent to do fewer things well than many things poorly?"

Jun Li looked out to the Huangpu River, waiting for his father's response. There were knots of self-reproach in his stomach, but his father was never one to speak without considering his words. It took a few minutes.

"You seem to be crediting me with building an empire by myself. I had your mother. Your aunts and uncles. I had *you*. Would we have anything in Canada if you hadn't driven those investments? You're a strong leader, Jun Li. Ambitious and capable. The way you've stepped into my shoes makes me very proud, but I never ran this alone the way you do. I supported the expansion because it was what you wanted. I will always stand behind you. You're my son."

The back of Jun Li's throat grew tight, partly from his father's willingness to support his decision, which was a relief, but more from the sentiment in them. They weren't a family that used the word *love* openly, but when his father said, "You're my son," that's what he was saying. *I love you.* Jun Li heard it clear as a gong that reverberated in his ears.

For a few seconds, all he could think was that he had said the same to Ivy more than once. *You're my wife.* It was a different type of love to his father's for him, but that's what it was. Deep, enduring love.

"Your cousin would like a more prominent role," his father mused. "Perhaps rather than sell off those divisions, move them under a different banner and give her the role of president. Keep it in the family, at least."

"That's a good idea." Jun Li came back and retook his seat, mind quickly seeing the potential. They discussed it further, then he called Ivy. "I'd like to run up to Beijing to see my cousin. Will you be all right without me for a few more hours?"

For a moment, Ivy couldn't speak. When she drew a breath, it broke slightly. He heard it.

"You're crying." His voice gentled. "I'll leave now and come straight home."

"No. I was just speaking to Dad," she admitted.

"You're homesick? Did you tell him to come? I'll arrange it."

"He's going to call my assistant." She wasn't homesick. That was the problem. She had realized the place she thought of as home was wherever her husband happened to be. Jun Li had become her world.

It made her realize she had not become the woman she had aspired to be when she had had her affair with him. For a brief time, she'd been self-possessed and capable of creating happiness for herself, not relying on a man to provide it to her. She had promised herself she wouldn't fall for a man who didn't love her, but she had. She was both desolate and deliriously happy.

The worst part was, Jun Li deserved her love. He was considerate and respectful, and when she reached for him in the night, he took her hand and kissed her knuckles, silently reassuring her that she wasn't alone in the dark.

She was trying to understand how detached and untethered he must have felt all those years, suffering in silence, alone in a country that wasn't home. He'd been betrayed at a young age, too. She didn't want to pressure him to feel things that didn't come naturally, but she couldn't deny that she was hurting right now. She needed a little time to put herself back together before he came home.

"I'm fine," she lied. "Just wishing the aspirin was doing a better job with my headache. The midwife is coming soon. I'll ask her if I can take anything else. Then I'll have a nap and won't even notice you're not home yet."

"All right. Text me if anything changes."

"I will."

"Ivy—" He cut himself off.

"Yes?"

There was a lengthy silence where she heard her own pulse in her ears.

"I'll tell you when I get home," he said in a voice she'd never heard. It was tender and strong and wedged itself against her heart. "I'll be back before you go to bed."

"Is that supposed to be funny?" she asked with mock ire.

He gave a dry chuckle.

Another silence fell between them, one that acknowledged the distance between them. She wanted to say *Come home*. Not because she was scared or lonely or feeling less than one hundred percent. She was all those things, but she wanted to be with him. *I need you.*

Don't be that person, she admonished herself.

"The midwife is here," she said as the butler appeared at the door. "Travel safe. I love you."

"I'll see you soon."

Me too. That was what he should have said. *I love you, too.*

His heart was swelling like a balloon. A thousand thoughts and words had filled his throat, none of which did justice to the intensity of what he was experiencing. He had swallowed it back, wanting to get it right. He might not be the most romantic man in the world, but he thought the first time he opened his heart to his wife, he ought to do it in person.

He ended the call, and the glow that her voice had instilled in him continued to warm him as he continued with his day.

Four hours later, he shook his cousin's hand. She was smiling broadly, excited for the prospect of new responsibilities. He wanted to caution her to be careful what she asked for, but he was feeling too lighthearted. He was more optimistic than he'd been in a long time.

He was considering the best way to tell Ivy. He couldn't claim he had done this entirely for her. It was for himself and his own sanity, but also for *them*. For their growing family.

Deep down, he hoped she would see it as the grand gesture a man made when he wanted the woman he loved to know how deep his feelings ran. He wanted her to know that she was his priority. His everything.

He said his goodbye to his cousin and turned to the door as his assistant rushed in from ordering the helicopter. His face was pale, his voice urgent. He thrust out his phone.

"Sir. A message about your wife. She's had a seizure. The ambulance is on its way to the house."

CHAPTER TWELVE

"IT WAS VERY SUDDEN," the midwife told him as she escorted him to the maternity ward. "I put the fetal heart rate monitor on her in the afternoon and came back a few hours later to check it. The baby was not in distress, but her blood pressure had gone up. I said we should go to the hospital as a precaution. She wanted to call you, but before she could pick up the phone… Thankfully, she was on the bed and didn't fall. They delivered by surgery and it went well. She's in critical care. Your son is doing very well."

She took him into a nursery, where most of the babies were in open cradles, but she led him to the impossibly small, black-haired infant wearing only a diaper as he sprawled on his back in an enclosed unit.

"He's breathing on his own but getting a

little oxygen as a precaution. He doesn't have much body fat, so we're keeping him warm. Those wires are monitors, again for precaution. Would you like to touch him?"

Jun Li was numb from the anxiety of his travel here and felt split in half as he washed his hands. Mentally, he was racing through the corridors in search of Ivy. He'd nearly had a stroke when he got the news about her seizure. He wouldn't be able to breathe properly until he'd seen her and reassured himself she was all right.

The other half of him was here, taking in a miracle that put tears of gratitude in his eyes. How had he been afraid of what it meant to be a father? He knew exactly what he needed to do. He had to reassure his son that he was here. That all would be well.

As he reached through the aperture, his hand shook. It looked ridiculous, like the meaty paw of a giant as he ever so gently let it come to rest on his son's warm, bare belly, careful not to dislodge the stub of his umbilical cord. His new, thin skin was softer even than Ivy's cheek.

As Jun Li touched him, the boy's limbs seemed to fold in like a flower to clutch at his hand. It was reflexes—Jun Li knew that in his rational mind. In his heart, it was the yearning of a child to be held safely by its parent.

I'm here. I will always protect you, he silently promised.

He leaned his free arm on the top of the warming unit and rested his forehead on his wrist, breathing against the glass as he gazed on his son. He had Ivy's mouth, as if he needed anything more to imprint himself on the center of Jun Li's heart. The rise and fall of his tiny belly against his palm was timed to the heavy drum of Jun Li's heart in his chest.

This baby shouldn't have even happened. The forces that had come together to make him were impossible odds, yet here he was. He was a gift from a benevolent god. The link that had pulled Ivy's life into his own, joining them forever. He was so grateful for that. So grateful.

"Does he have a name?" the midwife asked gently.

He and Ivy had discussed several, but he refused to make that decision without her.

I have to find your mother. I'll be back. I love you.

Jun Li left a piece of his heart in the enclosure as he withdrew his hand and straightened.

"I need to see my wife."

"Blossom. My heart, my sunshine, my soul. Come back to me. You know I need you."

Ivy smiled in her sleep, not wanting to wake, because in her dream Jun Li was finally saying the things she had longed to hear.

"Destiny brought us together, Ivy. Fate. That is not something you can sleep through."

"I know you can hear me. You're smiling. Don't you want to see our son? Open your eyes."

Her hand was lifted, which somehow dragged

her the final distance out of her heavy sleep and forced her to blink her eyes open.

Jun Li held her knuckles against his mouth. His expression shone with such emotion, such love, her vision immediately blurred with tears.

"I want you to stop scaring years off my life. Do you think you can do that?" he asked with gentle humor. "Because I want as much time as possible with you."

"Is—" She moved her free hand to her empty belly, discovered she was wearing an IV wire on that hand. She was in a hospital. "Did you say son?"

"Yes. He's small but strong and fierce and beautiful. A quiet little fighter, like his mother. Do you know how much I love you, Ivy?"

"No." *Yes.* She could see it gleaming in his eyes. It went into her like a force that scattered light and joy within her, making her feel so special and precious, she wanted to close her eyes against it. It was almost too much to bear, being loved this hard by this man.

"I should have been here." His regret was palpable.

"You're here now." She really should have paid attention to the fact he had always been there in the ways that counted. She swallowed the knot that formed in her throat.

"I'll be here more." He released her hand to lower the rail. He hitched his hip onto the bed beside her, then took up her hand again. "When I left to see my father, I was only thinking of how much you were doing for me—having our baby no matter what it cost you. How could I ever match that? I wanted to show you how much you matter."

"What did you do?" she asked with a trace of apprehension.

"Nothing drastic. I canceled the aeronautics expansion and restructured so my cousin will take a large chunk of responsibility off my plate."

"Oh, is that all," she said with a bewildered laugh.

"I wanted you to know how much you and our son mean to me. Then I wasn't here when you needed me. It will be a long time before I forgive myself for that."

"I don't remember any of it," she assured him. "I'm guessing you wouldn't have been able to do anything. I needed a doctor." She gently palpated her belly through the bandages, discovering the tender spots. Her head was spinning as she tried to absorb all he was saying. "But… Jun Li, I don't need gestures. I mean, I love that you'll have more time with us, but words are enough. I know you wouldn't say them unless they were true."

"They are true, but they're not enough." He gave his head a solemn shake. "I love you in ways that are so new, so complex, I didn't know what I was feeling. I fought examining it." He caressed her cheek with the backs of his fingers. "As if I could avoid the potential for pain if I didn't acknowledge how much you meant to me. But these last hours… The thought of losing you is beyond what I can bear, Ivy. I love you with all my heart." He leaned forward and kissed her in a soft benediction. A seal of the words scrolled across their hearts.

"I love you, too," she said when he lifted his

head. She set her hand against his unshaven cheek. His eyes were deeply set and bruised with lack of sleep. Lines of stress were scored next to his mouth. He was still preposterously beautiful. "I would like to circle back to this and kiss you a few thousand more times, but… Can I see our son first?"

Six weeks later, Ivy was about to rise and take Li Qiang back to his room when Jun Li came into their darkened bedroom.

"You're home." She hadn't expected him until tomorrow afternoon.

"We finished early." He spoke quietly as he came to steal Li Qiang. "And I missed you. Both of you," he whispered and kissed the baby. "Were you taking him back to bed? I'll do it."

Ivy snuggled under the covers, drowsy since it was after midnight, but listening on the baby monitor as Jun Li briefly spoke to the nanny and settled their son with tender words for the boy.

When he came back, he dragged off his tie

and shirt, throwing all his clothes to the floor as he undressed for bed. He'd been in Beijing for three days, finalizing the restructuring.

Ivy had stayed home because she had had a doctor's appointment and a million other things to organize. They had spoken daily, mostly about Li Qiang and the various details for their upcoming travel and move. With Jun Li's cousin taking over most of the operations based here in Shanghai, she and Jun Li were spending Christmas with Ivy's father, who had put off his wedding until she could attend. Afterward, they would decamp to Singapore, where Jun Li would be closer to the port construction and other projects he would oversee for the next few years.

Ivy had agreed to chair the committee that organized the annual strategy meeting there. It was a good way to get to know more about the company and see where she might fit at some future point. She had also reached out to some of her contacts asking if there was work she might do piecemeal. She wasn't in a hurry to go back to work, especially not full-time, but she wanted to keep her hand in.

Jun Li lifted the blankets and slid in, gathering her to his naked body.

"Oh," she said with disappointment.

"I only want a kiss," he said, drawing back. They had fooled around a little in the last few weeks but hadn't made love since she'd been put on bed rest three months ago.

"No, um, I bought something. I should have changed into it while you were putting Li Qiang down. I didn't think of it until I realized what I was wearing."

"Something?" he prompted.

"Something better than a nursing nightgown and sleep bra. Something I was going to put on when we got to Vancouver, to see if I could improve your opinion of my hometown." She lightly pinched his flat stomach, and he caught her hand.

"Describe it." He brought her hand to his mouth and scraped his teeth against the heel of her palm. "In detail."

"I should start with the price, because it was outrageous considering what little I got."

"Less is more. Everyone knows that. Expense approved. Keep talking."

"There's no garter belt. I hope that doesn't upset you. I got the kind of stockings that stay up on their own so I could keep them on... Mmm."

He rolled her beneath him as he covered her mouth, kissing her hungrily.

Oh, it felt good to feel his weight, his skin, his *hardness*. She scraped her nails lightly against his buttocks, and he groaned and nibbled at her chin.

"Color?" he asked against her throat.

"Purple. I got the size wrong and the bra cup is too small."

"An understandable mistake to make." He gathered her breast, gently massaging through the layers of cotton she wore. "You're forgiven."

"The panties are barely a fig leaf on a satin thread."

"Maybe better suited to tangling around

your wrists?" He caught her hands and swept them under the pillow.

A streak of excitement hit her belly, thrilling and hot.

"Tell me there are slippers with a four-inch heel and feathery pom-poms on the toe."

"I'll buy some," she assured him. "There's a sheer nightgown that goes over it. It's *very* short."

"Good, because this one is too long and has to come off." He gathered a handful and started to tug it up.

She wiggled to help, and he flung it away while she wrestled herself free of her bra and plain cotton underpants.

"There is one more thing we have to talk about," she said as their naked bodies brushed deliciously against one another's.

"If you tell me there's some sort of elbow-length gloves, I may not last to finish what we're starting. I have really missed this, blossom. Really. *Really.*"

She could tell. She smiled into the dark and opened her legs so he nestled his erection against her soft, damp folds. She draped her arms around his shoulders and caressed the back of his neck.

"I made a decision without your input," she informed him. And she was aware he could make his own decisions without her having a say, but she hoped he agreed with hers. "I asked the doctor to give me an IUD. I know you said you would have another vasectomy and didn't want to put me through another pregnancy, but I don't want to close the door on having another baby. Not yet."

"Your body, your choice," he said promptly. Then kissed her. "I wasn't ready to close that door, either. Thank you for leaving it open for both of us."

"For all we know, it's wide-open." She twined her legs up to his waist. "Does birth control even work for us?"

"I guess we'll see."

"I guess we will."

EPILOGUE

"PLEASE, MAMA?" Li Qiang placed a hand on her knee and tilted his head appealingly. "I really want a sleepover."

He had only learned the word three seconds ago, but he was deeply sincere and, unbeknownst to him, breaking his parents' hearts by appearing so willing to have a night apart from them.

"I think we'll play until bedtime, then go back to our hotel." Ivy stroked his hair to cushion the blow. "You and Mimi have time to finish your puzzle." She nodded at the giant floor puzzle Li Qiang was assembling with Kevin and Carla's daughter.

Mimi had been conceived on the couple's honeymoon and had been born only a few months after Li Qiang. The pair got on like a house on fire.

"But why?" He turned to his father and tilted his head. "Bàba, please?"

Why was Li Qiang's favorite word these days, but that wasn't what made Carla and Kevin bite back grins. Li Qiang, their late talker, had spent a full three years pointing and grunting and only using a handful of words. As a preemie, certain delays were to be expected, but the speech therapist had said he was also probably confused.

Initially, Ivy and Jun Li had made the decision that Ivy would read to him in English while Jun Li read the stories in Mandarin. They spoke to each other in whichever language the words came to them but decided to focus strictly on Mandarin until he started to speak.

The day Ivy had picked up a Mandarin book, Li Qiang had said clear as day, in English, "That one is Bàba's. I get *Goodnight Moon*."

From then on, he had been speaking nonstop. The funny part was, he spoke to Ivy in English and Jun Li in Mandarin. Her father always greeted Li Qiang in Cantonese over the tablet, so now that was "their talk."

Kevin was highly amused by it and had tried to confuse Li Qiang by throwing out the little Hokkien he knew. The joke was on him—that was the nanny's first language, and Li Qiang knew more than Kevin did.

"Come." Jun Li invited Li Qiang into his lap. "What happens if you need us in the night? We don't want to be so far away." To the adults, Jun Li added, "I've never understood the North American obsession with sleepovers."

Kevin barked out a laugh. "This from the man who let me sleep over for two years?"

"It was your home," Jun Li corrected with a small frown of annoyance. "We were roommates."

"Well, my home is your home, and we'll always have a bed for you here. You can all stay the night. How's that?" Kevin asked. "We could do calculus homework like old times."

"Tempting," Jun Li said dryly and looked to Ivy.

"The children are playing so nicely," she pointed out.

Jun Li put Li Qiang onto his feet and said, "We will all have a sleepover, then."

Li Qiang and Mimi ran back to their puzzle, giddy with excitement.

"The appeal of sleepovers," Kevin said as though explaining it to a simpleton, "is that you get your child out of your bed for a night so you can make another one."

"I'll take that under advisement," Jun Li said blandly while Ivy looked into her soda water with lime.

They were ahead of the curve on that one. A month ago, after much discussion, she'd had her device removed. She'd fallen pregnant laughably fast, so they'd booked this trip. Hopefully there wouldn't be any complications this time around, but they were putting a plan in place in case she was put on bed rest again and were getting all their overseas visiting done early.

Some hours later, when Ivy was spooned into her husband's body, replete from their lovemaking, she sensed a lingering tension that wasn't allowing him to fall asleep.

"He's across the hall," she murmured. "Go check on him if it will make you feel better."

"I just want to hear him if he calls out."

Just then, little feet padded up to the door and the latch rattled. "Mama?"

Jun Li rose before she could and stepped into his boxers while she sat up to pull on her nightgown. He unlocked the door and picked up Li Qiang.

"What's wrong? Bad dream?"

"I missed you."

"You did? Well, it's a good thing we're here, then." He closed the door and brought their son to bed. "Your feet are freezing. You missed putting them on me, didn't you?"

There was some giggling and wiggling as they all made themselves comfortable.

Jun Li reached across their son to set his hand on her hip. "*Now* I can sleep," he said around a big yawn.

Ivy smiled in the dark. "I love you, you know."

"I love you, too."

"And me," Li Qiang said.

"And you too."

Life wasn't perfect. Both she and Jun Li knew that. He was off his medication, but he might need it again sometime. Her pregnancy could be difficult, and any of their parents could suffer a downturn in health.

That's why they had agreed that when a moment was as blissfully perfect as this one, they had to acknowledge and treasure it.

"Thank you for what we have," she said, searching out his face in the dark so she could caress his cheek. "I'm really happy right now."

"Me too, blossom." He kissed the inside of her wrist. "Me too."

* * * * *